VICTORY GARDEN

A NOVEL

MEREDITH ALLARD

Copperfield
PRESS

Two roads diverged in a wood, and I…
   I took the road less traveled by,
   And that has made all of the difference.

~Robert Frost

PROLOGUE

$\mathcal{I}$ was there that day at the White House in 1917, just before the war. We had gone to Washington to ask for the assistance we were promised when Mr. Woodrow Wilson was campaigning to become the next President of the United States. Then, Wilson considered women's influences important, worthy of courting and pandering to. He knew he could alienate potential future women voters by not showing interest in our suffrage cause. Wilson said if he were elected President, if the women did their part to influence their fathers, husbands, and sons into voting for him, he would make votes for women a reality. After Wilson was inaugurated in 1912, we were nuisances, no longer worthy of acknowledgment. But we wanted what we had been promised, which was presidential aid in making woman suffrage a reality. We wanted our voices heard. We wanted our freedom and our choices.

We weren't whole citizens. We couldn't vote. How could we find equality in a society that wouldn't grant us our rights? Wilson said he didn't remember his election promises, which is the way of most politicians. But we would no longer allow ourselves to be unremembered. We had been unremembered 70 years by then.

Past the green, flowering lawns and the black, wrought-iron gates, inside the pristine, colonial walls of the White House, we were shown into a reception room by a blank-faced attendant who hardly noticed the dozen women before him. We seated ourselves in the chairs set out in neat, school-like rows, with one chair up front for Teacher, as though the People's House were transformed into a school for impudent girls. We removed our low-lying hats, tugged off our gloves, and then we were told to wait by an over-tired, over-burdened aide who bustled in and scurried out with more important things on his mind. We smoothed our ankle-length skirts and set our faces.

"The President is very busy," the bustling man said when he returned and saw us still waiting. "America will be at war soon. There will be blood and battles, soldiers and death. This will be a show of fortitude, of *man*power, and we can no longer isolate ourselves in the world. The President doesn't have time for women's issues today."

"But we don't need guns or bombs or blood-won trenches to make our point, sir," Lucy Burns said. "We have determined women willing to wait so their daughters and granddaughters will no longer have to."

"You'll have to wait a while," the fidgety man said. "At least until the war is over. This is a time of supreme importance for America. This is our time to propel ourselves into greathood. This is our time to achieve our most worthy ideals of democracy and freedom for the world's encumbered. There are people who are oppressed in the world."

"We are oppressed in the world," Lucy Burns said.

"There are whole countries with whole languages with whole peoples suffering from the oppression of misguided imperialism. We're going to join this European war, and we're going to free the people of the world, and we're going to put ourselves on the highest rung of the earth's ladder. We'll triumph over evil. So, you see, President Wilson is busy. He cannot see you today."

Lucy Burns stood and addressed the man directly.

"He has promised to see us for days, months even. Do men not elect presidents who keep their promises?"

"He is busy with pressing matters."

"We are pressing matters."

"He is dealing with matters of whole-world importance."

"Then we will wait."

Her rusted red hair nearly matched the intensity of her eyes and the glow of her skin. Lucy Burns wasn't bitter in her tone. She wasn't angry or forlorn. She sat as the aide left the room.

"We will wait," she said again. We will wait because it is our fate to wait. He has promised to hear us and we will wait until he does. We have stories to tell and songs to sing. We have been waiting long for acknowledgment and understanding.

We will wait our whole lives, just as our mothers waited their whole lives, as our grandmothers waited their whole lives, and their mothers and grandmothers before them, waiting whole human lifetimes as far back as existence can recall. All along we have been waiting our turn. We will still wait, only now we will be visible. You will see us waiting.

When the aide passed through some time later and found us still there, he shook his head and backed away, disappearing into antiques and tapestries. I sat close to the window, and as I put my white gloves on I saw the black automobile with the straight-sitting chauffeur and the President, dressed in gray, proper, narrow, unblinking under his owl-eyed rims. His gaze focused nowhere, his expression revealed nothing as the car sputtered passed the White House gates. Next to me was my aunt, Cynthia Wilcox, with whom I shared my suffragist tendencies, and together we watched the car disappear down the drive. She brushed some auburn hair from my eyes, took my white-gloved hands in hers, and sighed.

"We won't see the President today, Rose," she said.

"Another day, Miss Scofield," Lucy Burns said as she walked past me. "We will see the President another day."

We gathered our parasols and our handbags, adjusted our hats, and left escorted by guards from the White House grounds.

CHAPTER 1

*T*he first time I saw him I wasn't thinking of verdigris eyes that only smiled, of a fulfilled life that understood love, of glee-filled laughter or soul-filled piano music. The first time I saw him, I was thinking about vaudeville.

It was April 1917 when my father brought me to a vaudeville theater off-Broadway—a dark, gas-lit room that didn't know electric lighting was the vogue. The previous audience was leaving, a collection of working-class families, nursing mothers, young people out for an evening of cheap entertainment, and children, many children, making room for the evening patrons who listened for the scoop on the acts. Houdini had played there, and on their way out the audiences raved. Occasionally, an outstanding act would rise from beneath the rubble of boring, badly sung songs or lazy, badly stepped dances, though the problem with vaudeville, as with most entertainment, was that audiences were so used to seeing the bad that the bad began to look good. Still, they listened for some clue about who was to appear that night, and the audiences gladly paid their nickels and dimes in hopes of accidentally sitting in on a quality show.

My father showed his press credentials to the usher taking

tickets at the door, and we were shown to seats in the center of the third row. As we squeezed ourselves between some rambunctious children, my father explained why he had to see this show.

"You see, Rosie," he said, his slate-gray eyes that matched my own gleaming in the gas light, "yesterday this young man pushes his way past Beatrice into my office. 'Mr. Scofield,' the kid says, 'I'm Max Bell, and I'm gonna let you in on an act that's taking the world by storm.'

"The kid sticks a stogie thicker than three of his fingers into his mouth and slaps a black scrapbook on my desk. He opens the book to show me photographs and newspaper clippings from some vaudeville. 'My brothers and I work together in an act called the Five Bell Brothers,' the kid says. 'I want you should look at these reviews. Good reviews we've got, lots of them, and audiences all over the country who come to see us whenever we're in town. We've been playing the small-time circuits for years, but we're ready for the Big Time.'"

The cerise curtains went up and the first act of acrobats filled the stage. My father lowered his voice to a whisper.

"'We could get to the Big Time if we had the right reviews,' Max said. 'You're a respected man from the *New York Times*, Mr. Scofield. One good word from you and people will listen. We want you should see our act tomorrow night, then give us a write-up in your column, one that will get us into the Big Time. Well? Hells bells! What do you say?'"

My father laughed. "How could I refuse such a request?"

He glanced at the brightly colored acrobats tumbling across the stage while two men in court jester attire juggled apples and oranges, then flaming watermelons painted like the Stars and Stripes for a finale. My father shook his head as if he didn't care for what he saw. This first act was known as the doormat act, the one that filled the stage while the late coming audience arrived— an unwelcome task.

I wasn't impressed, either, and I watched the crowd, mostly

working-class, mostly immigrant, loud and uninterested in the acrobats tumbling or the jugglers juggling. These were faces of people tired from working long hours for little wages, who wanted to forget their days in song, dance, and laughter, who wanted to see themselves reflected back in a way they could take with them when they returned down the unlit alleys to their homes where they escaped until the sunlight brought another welcomeless day. If their nickels and dimes bought a respite from what waited for them outside, they walked away happy.

The acrobats and jugglers finished their opening number, disappearing into the wings. The loud-chatting audience hardly noticed that the curtain dropped. A moment later the curtain rose to reveal six ballerinas, and whoops and hollers came from those inclined to show their appreciation that way. The ballerinas toe-danced in tulle and ribbons of red, white, and blue while the marching tones of "Yankee Doodle" rose from the five musicians in the orchestra pit.

My father watched the ballerinas twirling their American flags and he grimaced. "President Wilson is intent on declaring war," he said. "Now he wants to convince the country that joining the war in Europe is the only way we can preserve democracy."

"At first he was reluctant to send American troops into a European war," I said. "When we were in Washington we realized he changed his mind. Now he sees America as the savior of all nations."

"He's trying to inspire the Patriotism to promote his cause—100% Americanism." My father shook his head as he looked at the red, white, and blue streamers dangling from the stage. "It looks like vaudeville has already caught the Patriotism."

"The Patriotism. You make it sound like the plague."

"You wait and see."

We watched the dancers lead each other off the stage, arm in arm, toes in sync. The curtain went down and up again and the emcee introduced the next act—a dramatic skit with men in tights and ladies in skirts and bodices. Then, according to the emcee, was the first corker of the night, the first big punch of the show. The audience in its collective glee leaned forward, clapping and hollering. No longer interested in the sight of the audience or the act on the stage, I leaned back against my seat and closed my eyes, trying to ignore the snickers and hoots from those who were also bored but less shy about showing it. I tried to forget how enclosed I felt sitting amongst so many people. I didn't want to feel claustrophobic the way I did whenever I felt surrounded, as if there were no way out. I didn't like feeling trapped. Suddenly, I was warm and tired, and I fell asleep despite the chaos around me.

I was startled when my father shook me awake. I opened my eyes to see the audience filing into the aisles, chattering excitedly about what they saw.

"You missed the Five Bell Brothers," my father said, wiping away his happy tears. He took my hand and led me from the seats. "Come on, Rosie. I have to meet those boys. That was some of the best comedy I've seen in years."

I followed my father to the side door where he showed his press credentials. We stepped backstage where the glitter flashed like a kaleidoscope. I wanted to shield my eyes from the illuminations of the costumes, the jewelry, the brilliant smiles. Mostly the smiles were big and toothy, the forced kind you see when the inclination isn't to smile at all but to bolt out the door, away from the crowds that demanded, often impolitely, to be entertained for their money. But there was an ease of camaraderie amongst the entertainers as they joked and laughed with their arms around each other. They seemed comfortable together in New York, as they probably were in Kalamazoo, Wichita, San Francisco, and wherever else their vaudeville circuit brought them.

My father found an elegant, silver-haired gentleman carrying a ruby-studded walking stick and asked where he could find Max Bell and his brothers. The gentleman gibbered joyfully in a language neither my father nor I understood. The man gestured for us to follow him, and with his walking stick he cut through the cigarette smoke and pushed aside the heated bodies, the props, and the posters until we arrived in an unventilated room where some of the performers were intent on a poker game. Suddenly, a dark-haired young man wearing a white duck suit, a thick black cigar hanging from his lips, stood and pointed at another player.

"Hells bells! Pay up already, will you?"

My father smiled. "That's Max." I loved it when something caught the magic in my father's eyes and made him light up pink like the wide-eyed boy he still could be. The loss of my mother to consumption, the political corruption of Tammany Hall, the fall of Theodore Roosevelt from the heights of political prowess, the rise of women and children sweatshop labor, the city congestion where everyone who drove a motor car thought he was the reason for the roads, with robbery, rape, and murder on the rise—all of it meant my father was no longer as serene as he had once been. I loved him for his concern for others, and I loved him even more for his desire to spoil the follies of mankind in his newspaper columns. I was grateful to whoever these Five Bell Brothers were for whatever they did to grant him this time away from the worries of the world.

Max Bell approached us, winking at my father. "Lie to you, did I, Mr. Scofield?"

"You did not," my father answered.

"Entertained you, did we?"

"Yes, you did, my boy. Yes, you did."

"Then you're going to write a good review for us, right?"

"You'll be on the Big Time if I have anything to say about it."

Max nodded while he looked me up and down. "You know her?" Max nodded in my direction.

"Only her whole life."

Max smiled a polite smile for my father, a different smile for me, then disappeared. As my father and I turned to leave, our path was blocked by a human obstacle course. There, on their knees, gesticulating with open arms toward me, their faces caught between instantaneous love and playful admiration, were five young men in white duck suits, including Max, who had to be brothers.

I was abashed by such rapt attention from these men I didn't know, even if they were pleasant looking. I didn't know what to do or how to respond, so I stared with an embarrassed grin at waves of dense, unwieldy hair that ranged from chestnut to sepia and large, amused eyes that ranged from verdigris-green to gray-blue. My next reaction was to ignore them, but there was no ignoring the Five Bell Brothers. The less I tried to notice them the wider their gesticulating, and the wider their gesticulating the less I tried to notice them. When I thought I would explode from distress, one of the brothers stepped closer, inspecting me.

"Hey!" he said, his voice pleasant and mellow. "You're the dame who slept through our whole act!"

My cheeks flushed and my stomach burned. "Why, yes," I said.

"Don't worry about it, though you're the only one I've ever known to sleep through a vaudeville except the performers."

"I don't know," said Max. "After all, you did sleep during our act right through to the end." He turned to his brothers. "I think she owes us a better apology than that."

"You took that much notice of me?" I asked.

"Certainly," Max said. "I always notice the pretty dames in the audience."

"Yah," said the brother who had first spoken, "especially the unconscious ones. He's met some of his best dates that way."

Max leaned close to me. "Say, you wouldn't like to meet up after the show and…"

"What about Mary Lou?" asked another brother.

"Mary Who?"

"Not Mary Who. Mary Lou. You know, the poor girl who thinks you're going to marry her one day."

"You mean Mary Boo Hoo."

"That's the one."

The brothers were no more than overgrown boys. At first, I found their comfortable mannerisms bothersome, though in a matter of moments, touched by their friendliness, I found them endearing. They were hurricanes, the Bell Brothers, five distinct, individual hurricanes, blowing and huffing about simultaneously, encircling and encompassing everyone around them. The smoke from their cigars or cigarettes permeated everything. Their voices, though some were deeper or smoother or louder or slower, were everywhere. They talked at the same time, smoked at the same time, laughed at the same time, and flirted at the same time.

Max called to his brothers. "Hey, boys! I forgot to introduce you to Mr. Scofield here. He's the nice man who's going to write the review that's going to get us into the Palace."

"That big one in England?" asked a younger brother.

Max shook his head. "You'll have to excuse my brother Jacob. He fell on his head when we were in Pittsburgh."

"I didn't fall. I was dropped."

Max looked sideways at his brother. "I haven't introduced you to my herd here, Mr. Scofield. Bell boys to attention! Roll call!" The brothers popped into line, army-style. "Here we are in the order of appearance that pleased Mother but surprised the hell out of Pop. Stuart!"

Stuart took a step forward. "I'm the oldest and Stuart is next in line. He talks almost as fast as I do except I've had two more years of practice at it. He tells jokes in the act, and he even sings in his very own key. Adam!"

Adam was the brother who had first recognized me as the dame who slept through their act. "Adam plays the piano. I think he has another talent, but I can't tell you what it is."

The first thing I noticed when I looked at Adam Bell was his eyes—wide, green, and smiling. Stepping in front of his brothers, Adam bowed in a genteel manner toward my father and tipped his derby toward me, winking, not a leering, wicked wink but an amiable one, almost brotherly in its understanding.

"Jacob!"

The smallest of the brothers, Jacob nodded from where he stood. "He sings and plays the clarinet. We'd put him in the comedy act except he's never strung more than four words together in a sentence. Then there's David." Max pointed to the youngest of the brothers who looked no more than 15. "He's not too bright, but he sings well and carries our luggage wherever we go."

"I'm doing this until I can get a real job," David said.

"Hey," said Stuart, "this is a real job."

Adam laughed. "Yah," he said. "Too bad it doesn't pay real money."

"Does this line of work pay well?" my father asked.

"Let's put it this way," Max said. "We don't know if we're going to sleep in a hotel room until we see how much dough we pulled in that night. We make our real money at the poker table, or pool, whichever we can find action at first, except for Jakey there who'd rather play with himself."

"I play solitaire," Jacob said.

"That's one way to play with yourself," said Max.

"Hey!" said Adam. "There's a lady here."

Max bowed. "I beg of you a hundred pardons, Miss Scofield. I didn't mean to offend you."

"It's all right, Mr. Bell," I said. "I'm not so easily offended."

My father began to question Max about the dollars and cents side of small-time vaudeville, to which Max answered there were few dollars to be had and even less sense. The conversation turned to the next poker game, and my father, who was known to sit in for a few hands now and again, was interested in where and when. Behind me I noticed a sign that warned the performers to make certain their acts appealed to the widest audiences:

Don't say 'slob' or 'son of a gun.'

Don't say 'holy gee.'

Don't say 'hell,' 'damn,' 'devil,' 'cockroach,' or 'spit.' Any act found uttering anything sacrilegious or suggestive will be immediately closed. It is worse to offend than to have no talent.

Adam Bell stood beside me, careful to blow his cigarette smoke away from my face. "I guess we're safe," he said. "We don't offend and we have no talent."

"My father thinks differently," I said.

Adam crunched his cigarette beneath his boot and leaned against the wall, his hands in his pockets. "When you said you weren't so easily offended you meant it."

"I did."

He smiled, a huge, pleasing smile. "Yah, I could tell. I knew I liked you even if you did sleep through our act." He nodded his head at the sign on the wall. "Can you believe how closely they watch us? Say one wrong thing and you're closed out of that circuit for months."

"Have the Five Bell Brothers ever been closed out for saying the wrong thing?"

"Once or twice—a month, that is, always because of Max. He's a fast talker, all right, which helps to get us gigs but it also gets us closed out."

Adam excused himself and returned to his brothers. I left for home on my father's arm without understanding what had happened.

CHAPTER 2

*T*he following afternoon I walked home from the school where I taught first grade with a nickel in my pocket, searching the shops along the way for anything I might like to buy. Today a nickel is nothing, throwaway change, but in 1917 a nickel was a prized possession. Five cents could buy you a lukewarm glass of beer with a free lunch, a subway ride, or a Sunday newspaper with a comics section printed in color. A nickel could buy you a shave, a shoeshine, a sandwich, a pack of cigarettes, a ticket to the moving pictures, or a good cigar. A dinner with wine and music at an elegant restaurant cost one dollar. Macy's department store sold a gallon of 100-proof Mount Vernon Rye for two dollars. Bloomingdale's made a man's suit to order for thirteen dollars. Five years earlier Carl Jung had broken away from Freud's sexual interpretations of everything from women's purses to train tunnels, and in 1917 he published *Psychology of the Unconscious.* Moving pictures, glimmers of sentimentalized lives, devoid of sound or color, began replacing vaudeville as the entertainment of the masses. "Covent Garden: Ragtime Waltz" by Marcella Henry and "Shave 'em Dry" by Sam Wishnuff were popular tunes, Model-Ts the standard mode of transportation. But when we're living our lives we don't consider what we wear or what we do as the makings of posterity. Only later do we realize that we lived through extraordinary changes, and it's only afterward that we recognize that we've lost something in the translation from then to now—the ability to look around as if there were something new to discover each day.

I lived in New York City down a tree-lined neighborhood in a red-brown brownstone I shared with my father. I was a born New Yorker, a city girl in a time when American cities still felt new. I was at home among the electric lights, the skyscrapers, the crowds, the open-air automobiles that cranked and sputtered down the streets. In 1917, Manhattan played an unending vignette, color and drab, glamour and dilapidation, flamboyance and timidity, clutter and clatter. Model-Ts, Cadillacs, and Oldsmobiles, with their chugging, bulky masses, pushed their way through thin-winding roads, their drivers frustrated and flinching or bored and unconcerned as they missed colliding with other autos, low-flying birds, or the audacious pedestrians determined to make their way. Honking horns and loud voices, the thunder of the El trains pulled by locomotives that dropped sparks and cinders on the people lumbering beneath, screeching brakes, and laughing children were all set to the quick-time syncopation of ragtime music.

I was happiest inside the brownstone where there was the camaraderie that exists between people who are alone in the world and have pulled together to make it through. Where there was chaos out there, inside, where the floral-patterned over-stuffed furniture gave comfort, where birds chirped at the seeds and nuts left for them in dishes on the windowsill, where flowers grew in their small plot in the backyard, where the wind-up Victrola sent the joyous melodies of Mozart or the quick-time rhythms of Al Jolson into the air, there was rest for the weary. Whenever I walked into the brownstone again after even only an hour or two away, I exhaled in relief because it was good to be home. That afternoon, the nickel unspent and warm in my hand, I plopped onto the overstuffed armchair and closed my eyes. I needed some rest after a tiring day chasing after a roomful of seven-year-olds. Mrs. Harris, our housekeeper, her white frilly apron tied tightly around her ample waist, her graying hair tied into what she called a "hot cross bun," clapped her hands as she did every time I came home, as she had every time she saw me for as long as she had been working for us—nearly 20 years by then.

"Don't fall asleep now, Rose," she said, shaking my shoulder. "Your father is bringing home a guest for dinner. They'll be here any minute."

I stood from the chair, shaking away my lethargy. "Who?" I asked.

Mrs. Harris winked as though the answer was her secret. Then she leaned close and whispered, "A young man."

"Which young man?"

"I hardly know, Rose. Your father mentioned his name, but you know how I am about names." She pointed to her ear and laughed. "In one and out the other." She nudged me toward my bedroom. "Go spiffy yourself up, young lady. Take a bath and brush your hair. Put on that pretty lilac dress you wore to Mrs. Wilcox's dinner party last month. You looked lovely in that, the way it brought out the light in your eyes."

I glanced at myself in the gilded mirror on the wall. A few hairs had fallen from their upsweep, and the lines in my dress had flattened a bit during my busy day, but otherwise everything looked buttoned and fastened. "Do I look that bad?" I asked.

"You look a little wilted, Rose."

"I've been teaching seven-year-olds all day. If you did what I did you'd look a little wilted too."

"You don't need to work, Rose. Your father makes enough money at the *Times* to support you comfortably. You can leave that teaching nonsense alone and focus on your real work."

I smiled at Mrs. Harris. "Which is?"

Mrs. Harris slapped her hand in the air as though the answer were obvious. "What other job does a woman have? To find a husband! Which is why we need you to look your best tonight. It's not every evening an eligible young man shows up in your home."

"Did Dad say he was eligible?" I asked.

"He didn't say so specifically, no, but I'm sure the young man *must* be eligible. Why else would your father bring him here?"

I nodded, allowing Mrs. Harris to believe there was no other possible reason my father might bring home an unmarried man other than to be introduced to me. I didn't have it in me to remind her that she was the only one bothered by my unmarried status. I was all of 27 then, though in 1917 that was nearly, if not already, matronly. Still, I was one of the fortunate ones. I never felt pressure to do anything I didn't want to do from my father. He never pushed me this way or that, the way others would have me go. He taught me to know my own mind though we lived in a time when women's minds were thought too small, too frail for validation. He taught me to never settle for anything less than the rules of my own heart, and that it's worth the fight to live my life on my own terms. And I wanted to live according to my own terms, even if I wasn't yet sure what those terms might be. Then, like most women, I took it as my due that I must wait. Young women expected romanticized lives, Cinderella stories of passionate, soul-filled kisses and dewy, morning-filled eyes that flickered like the frames of the moving pictures that made the ordinary seem wonderful, perfect, too good to be true. And it was too good to be true, so I waited, content to wait, unlike Mrs. Harris, who was tired of my waiting.

As Mrs. Harris bustled back into the kitchen, rubbing her hands and laughing to herself as though she were plotting some cunning plan, I reached for the telephone and asked the operator for my aunt Cynthia's line. She wasn't only beautiful to look at, Cynthia, but she was socially elegant, a sought-after dinner guest by the elitist of the elite. She had the magic of small talk, which I did not, the ability to chat with anyone about anything. She would be my backup. She would know what to do.

THE YOUNG MAN in question was Montgomery Carter. Tall, dark-haired, muddy-eyed, at first glance he struck me as handsome if somewhat awkward in the way he held his neck long and his head high, as if the upper portion of his body were pulled upward by a rack, as if some thriving businessman were making a skyscraper out of him the way they were making skyscrapers out of every empty space in Manhattan. Mr. Carter arrived before my father, so it was Mr. Carter, Cynthia, and me while we waited. We sat on the overstuffed sofa in the sitting room while Mrs. Harris set out the dishes for dinner. Montgomery Carter was polite, if cold, when he had to respond to the harmless social niceties Cynthia posed to him as a way to draw him out of his shell.

"Martin said you're one of his new aides," she said.

"That's correct," answered the prim Mr. Carter.

"I know Martin is very happy to have you on board."

Cynthia paused, waiting for Mr. Carter to respond in kind as one would normally do in a conversation. When he stayed silent, eyeing the polished wood floor instead of answering, she tried again.

"Are you from New York?"

Montgomery turned to Cynthia, his expression aghast. "I am Montgomery Carter of the Fifth Avenue Carters. Yes, I am from New York."

The front door rattled and my father walked in—not a moment too soon, I thought. Cynthia was only too glad to give him her place next to Mr. Carter on the sofa. When her back was turned away from the men, she slapped her hand to her cheek and rolled her eyes. She followed me into the kitchen and together we burst out laughing very much at our guest's expense. Away from prying eyes, Cynthia stood straight, her head at an abnormally high angle, her little finger held awkwardly in the air as though she were sipping tea with the King, and said, in her most hoity-toity manner, "I am Montgomery Carter of the Fifth Avenue Carters. Yes, I am from New York."

I bowed toward her in my most genteel manner. "How do you do, Mr. Carter."

"I do better than you, thank you."

Mrs. Harris bustled in, checking the soup bubbling on the stove, pulling out the silverware from the drawer. She nudged me with her elbow as she stacked the silverware onto a platter.

"What do you think of him? He's very handsome. Dark hair. Dark eyes. Very mysterious looking, don't you think?"

"He's Montgomery Carter of the Fifth Avenue Carters," I said.

"Wealthy too? Rose, that's wonderful!" She lit up bright and clapped her hands under her chin as though Montgomery Carter and I were already engaged.

My father came into the kitchen, peeking under the lid of the pot on the stove. "Is dinner ready? I'm famished." He breathed in deeply. "Clam chowder, my favorite." He took a spoon from the counter, heading toward the pot until Mrs. Harris slapped his hand away.

"You can have a seat at the table," she said. "I'll bring the soup right now. That's a fine young man you brought here tonight, Mr. Scofield. Handsome and rich. Just the kind of man our Rose needs."

My father was appalled. "I didn't bring Montgomery here for Rose. I wouldn't let her marry him if he were the last man on earth. I don't care how much he stares at her picture on my desk."

Cynthia shook her head. "Martin…"

"Don't worry, Cynthia," my father said. "He might think Rose is pretty, which she is—the prettiest girl in town, just like her mother was, just like you—but we're not fancy enough for the Carters. I heard his mother has some toilet paper heiress set aside for him."

"I'm all right with not being fancy enough for Montgomery Carter," I said.

"Good girl," said my father.

Mrs. Harris bustled away with the white china soup tureen in her hands. "I don't know," she said. "Handsome, rich, available. Sounds like a catch to me. And Rose isn't getting any younger." She disappeared from the kitchen, and I threw my arms around my father's neck, kissing both of his cheeks.

"I love you for not bringing him here for me," I said.

"I love you too, Rose, which is exactly why I didn't bring him here for you."

"Then why did you bring him?" Cynthia asked.

"Mitchell Carter, Montgomery's father, is on the paper's board of directors. His wife asked me to take Montgomery under my wing, train him to become an editor, and teach him the newspaper business from the inside out. She said Montgomery was thirty years old and it's time he found some direction in his life. He started working for me this week, and I invited him here as a courtesy to Mrs. Carter, that's all."

Montgomery joined us at the dinner table, and Mrs. Harris brought out the wine. When Cynthia poured the first glass for our guest, he swirled it, first clockwise, then counterclockwise, and when he sniffed it I'm certain his nose crinkled and his lips puckered, if only for a moment until he could set his face to a more neutral expression.

"A unique vintage," Mr. Carter said. "I'm not familiar with it."

My father laughed. "It's a Merlot, circa 1917."

Mr. Carter wasn't much more talkative toward my aunt or me during dinner than he had been when he first arrived, even if he did occasionally sneak a glance in my direction, which I pretended not to notice. My father was right. We weren't fancy enough for a family like the Carters. While my father made a comfortable living at the *Times*, we were hardly wealthy. An ordinary middle-class girl, even if her father was a respected journalist, wouldn't be on any acceptable list to a polite family like the Fifth Avenue Carters. During dinner, Mr. Carter was attentive enough toward my father, so Cynthia and I sat back and listened while the men discussed newspaper business over clam chowder, dill-encrusted salmon, roasted potatoes, and a few more glasses of wine. The more Montgomery drank of the wine, the more agreeable it became to him.

We moved into the living room, and Mrs. Harris pulled my father aside to speak to him about some preparations for the dinner party we were having the following week. Cynthia stayed near to offer her advice, leaving Mr. Carter and me alone on the sofa in the living room. He glanced at me, then looked away, clearing his throat, pulling at his wide collar, and adjusting his jacket. Finally, he said, "I knew it was you as soon as I walked in. I've seen your photograph on your father's desk."

"I tend to look like my own photographs," I said.

Mr. Carter shook his head, not understanding. Finally, he managed a feeble smile. Then he nodded toward Cynthia. "Your mother is lovely."

"She's not my mother. She's my aunt, my mother's sister."

I looked at Cynthia, her heavy gold hair plaited high on her head, her sky-blue dress that brought out the silver in her eyes, her warm smile. I thought Cynthia and I didn't look alike at all though people said we did. Cynthia was a blond-haired, blue-eyed goddess, and I had auburn hair and slate-gray eyes like my father, though his red-brown hair was graying at the temples. Cynthia was tall and I wasn't. Everyone always said how beautiful my aunt was, and I agreed because she was. And then when they complimented my own looks, I didn't believe them. I always thought that if Cynthia was beautiful, and I didn't look like Cynthia, then I must not be beautiful. Mr. Carter must be fooled into thinking I look like my aunt, I thought, even with Cynthia standing nearby.

"Where is your mother?" Mr. Carter asked.

"She died when I was two," I said. I looked at Mr. Carter as he sat on the edge of the sofa, his back straight, his head high, and for the first time I noticed how deep-set his eyes were, how small. I waited for some acknowledgment of what I had shared, I just told him my mother died, but there was nothing. He didn't look concerned, he didn't look sad, and he didn't look like he cared to know when or where or why. I didn't want sympathy, but some reaction, some acknowledgment he heard me would have been nice. Even a simple "I'm sorry" would have been preferable to the silence. Mr. Carter's shoulders curled inward as he turned toward my father, who was still standing in the kitchen with Cynthia and Mrs. Harris. Mr. Carter tapped his foot while he waited for that conversation to finish.

"Pardon me," my father said as he joined us. "There was a mix-up with some details for a dinner party we're holding next week, but everything's settled now. I'm sure you understand about dinner parties, Montgomery."

"You must have the most fascinating parties, Mr. Carter," said Cynthia.

"We do," said the Fifth Avenue Carter. He leaned in my direction, his lips widening into what I guessed might be a smile. "I heard from your father you're part of the woman suffrage movement."

My father nodded, his pride in me evident in his gap-toothed grin. "That's right. Rosie here works closely with Mrs. Belmont to help the women of New York gain the vote."

Mr. Carter shook his head. "You're working to help women *gain* the vote? My mother helps the anti-suffrage movement. She thinks things should stay as they are."

"Things never stay as they are," Cynthia said. "Progress happens. Isn't it better to help progress along than to bury our heads in the sand and pretend the changes away?"

"If it isn't broken, don't fix it," Mr. Carter said.

"But the voting system is broken if half the population can't participate," I said.

Montgomery Carter nodded as though he were a parent lecturing an unreasonable child. "You do realize, Miss Scofield, there's a lot to consider when voting. You have to keep track of the various nominees and their platforms, and you have to decide what you believe, though I suppose most women would vote the way their fathers or husbands told them. Even so, there's a lot of responsibility that goes along with voting. If I were married, I wouldn't want my wife worried about things like voting when she needs to watch over my house and take care of my children."

"If you were married I would imagine your wife would have maids to care for the house and nannies to care for the children," I said.

"That's true, but it's the wife's responsibility to watch over the help and make sure they do their jobs. The wives are quite busy, I assure you, keeping after the maids and the cooks and the nannies and whoever else we have to assist us. There's little time to worry about voting."

"If I were married, Mr. Carter, I wouldn't want my husband thinking so little of my intellectual abilities that he didn't think I was capable of voting."

Mr. Carter shook his head. "If nothing else it must be an interesting way to bide your time."

"Bide my time?"

"Certainly. You need something to fill the hours of your day while you have nothing else to do. When you're married and have children you won't have time for such nonsense. Your priorities will be in your home with your family."

I stood from the sofa and paced to the other side of the room, afraid if I stayed where I was I'd strangle our guest with his own shirt collar, or at least scratch him a bit with my fingernails, preferably somewhere painful. I stood behind Cynthia, finding strength in her serene presence. She didn't seem flustered at all by Mr. Carter while I had to remove myself from his immediate vicinity so I wouldn't do him bodily harm. I glanced at my father, still mindful that Montgomery Carter was under his charge at the newspaper, but my father looked at his aide as though the young man were a stranger from another planet.

I sighed. "Mr. Carter," I said, "if I do marry and have children, I have no doubt they would be my main priority. But I would still make time for my suffrage work and other pursuits."

"What other pursuits?"

"Besides my work with the suffrage movement, I teach."

"What do you teach?"

"Rose teaches first grade at Mrs. Rittenhouse's school," my father said. "She's a wonderful teacher. Truly dedicated to her students."

"Mrs. Rittenhouse," Mr. Carter said, nodding. "I'm familiar with her. She runs a prestigious school." He turned to my father. "Even so, Mr. Scofield, do you think it's proper to allow your daughter to be out and about in the world that way, working like any common seamstress or washerwoman?"

My father closed his eyes and settled his temper the way I had a moment before. When he opened his eyes he was calm, smiling.

"Rose loves to teach," my father said.

Montgomery shook his head as though he had never encountered something so shockingly odd in all his days as a Fifth Avenue Carter. "I suppose teaching isn't a very difficult job," he said.

"I wouldn't suppose that at all," Cynthia said. She didn't have my father's spirit, as I did, so she remained as calm as ever. "You should see Rose's classroom. It's one of the most beautiful places I've been. Rainbow colors brighten the drab cast of the dull walls —rainbow colors in the children's art, rainbow colors on the birthday balloons, rainbow colors in the bookworm near the ceiling. She arrives early in the morning to prepare for the day and stays late into the afternoon to write her lessons."

"Do you enjoy teaching?" Mr. Carter asked.

"I love it. I love the children. I love decorating the room with the children's work so they can feel proud of what they've created. They ooh and aah when they see their work on the walls, and that's when they're truly learning. When I'm in my classroom I work with joy because there's nowhere else I'd rather be."

"That's lovely, Miss Scofield, but I return to my original point, which is that you would need to stop such nonsense if you were married."

"First of all, Mr. Carter, my teaching and suffrage work are not nonsense. Secondly, I won't stop teaching until I'm too old to keep going and I won't stop my suffrage work until the women of this country have the right to vote. I don't see why being a wife and mother means I can't have other dreams. I can't imagine a mother is any use to her children if she isn't happy with herself. Can you imagine being married to a woman who had no interests other than you? I'm sure you'd like it at first because you'd feel important. But then she'd bore you, then she'd annoy you, and then...?"

"Are you planning on marrying, Miss Scofield?" Mr. Carter asked.

"That's a rather personal question," I said.

"I apologize. I don't mean to pry. I'm curious, that's all."

I exhaled slowly through my mouth, my attempt to settle myself enough to answer using words that didn't include expletives. "I haven't decided if I want to be married, Mr. Carter. As it stands, I haven't found anyone I want to marry."

Mr. Carter nodded as though we were opponents across a chess table and I had called checkmate. My father changed the topic to some stories they were covering at the *Times*, and then Mr. Carter looked at the clock on the mantelpiece and said it was time for him to leave. I silently thanked the clock.

I followed my father as he showed our guest to the door. The men shook hands. Mr. Carter turned to me and said, "It was nice meeting you, Miss Scofield. You're even lovelier in person. I hope I'll have the pleasure of seeing you again soon."

My father grasped Montgomery's shoulder and pressed our

guest through the door toward the curb. When Cynthia closed the door behind them, she grinned at me.

"You have an admirer," she said.

I heard Mrs. Harris clap her hands from the dining room. "I knew it! I knew you two would be making eyes at each other before long. He's handsome, you're beautiful. You looked good sitting near each other, I have to say." She laughed as she disappeared into the kitchen. "And he's rich!" The door swung on its hinges and slapped Mrs. Harris on her ample behind.

I shook my head. "I'm not fancy enough for him. Remember?"

"We'll see," Cynthia said. She pulled aside the curtains and peeked at Mr. Carter as he stood near the expensive-looking black car talking to my father, the expensive-looking chauffeur waiting near the curb. My father and Mr. Carter shook hands again, and my father came back inside.

I didn't need to see. I had already decided. I didn't like Montgomery Carter. I didn't like his stiff posture. I didn't like the way he grimaced when he looked around the brownstone, and I certainly didn't like the way he was so dismissive of the suffrage movement, my teaching, and by extension, me. I said good night to my father and Cynthia, who remained huddled close on the sofa discussing Montgomery Carter. I locked myself in my room, trying desperately to forget I ever met the man.

CHAPTER 3

*T*he next morning the United States became a nation at war. The skyscrapers stood silent but watching over the people-crowded streets stretching from the waterways that came and went from far, far places. This was the day three years coming since the problems in Europe had grown beyond reason. This was what they had read papers for and asked questions about, and everyone pretended to have known all along that our boys would be going over there before long. Newspaper headlines proclaimed the sinking of the U.S. warship Aztec by the Imperial German government off the shores of Brest where 28 American lives were lost. It was too much to be endured. President Wilson had decided.

"Extra! Extra! Read all about it," shouted small-framed boys in oversized frock coats standing on the street corners, waving the newspaper at passers-by. "President Wilson asks war! American Armageddon!"

Months earlier President Wilson advocated a victoryless end to the imperialistic conflict that had already been raging war in Europe for three bloody years. Wilson called for an end without conclusions, an end without heroes. But neutrality was no longer good enough for him. Those of us who kept informed about world affairs had been aware of the growing tensions in Europe. The Sarajevo assassinations of Archduke Ferdinand and his wife made newspaper headlines in America for a day but were largely dismissed, then forgotten. Europe began the Great War in 1914, with England and France fighting off advancing German and Austrian armies. What had begun as a show of allegiance between countries escalated into modern warfare. In February 1917, with the war dragging on with no end in sight, the German government vowed to renew its unrestricted submarine warfare. An alarmed Wilson broke off diplomatic relations with Germany two days later.

In a special session of Congress, Wilson used his locution skills to convince the bipartisan Congress that this war was now a necessary evil for America. Observers said Wilson's speech lifted men's hearts and made them swell with national pride.

"The wrongs against which we now array ourselves are no common wrongs," Wilson said. "The world must be made safe for democracy."

When Jeanette Rankin, the only congresswoman, was called for her vote for or against the war, she clutched at her throat because that was where her heart was then. After she gave her "No" against American entrance into what was already known as the Great War, she slumped forward in her seat as though looking for the dreams of compassion that had gotten away. After her vote was made public, men gathered in the pubs, poked each other in the ribs, and said in their knowing voices that this was why women shouldn't be allowed to vote. They forgot that 49 others had also voted against the war, each of them men. But 373 representatives voted to join their Allies in France and bring victory home.

That morning was a busy city day like any other. People were everywhere, pushing their way down the sidewalk here, walking around you as if you were an inanimate obstacle there. On this new war morning the words, the honking horns, the voices, even the sparks and cinders falling from the El trains were tinged with the energy of a blossoming Patriotism. People looked happy this new war morning, relieved even. The men were dapper in duck suits, waistcoats, chains, and derbies. Women were weighed down by puff-shouldered blouses and long skirts, the girls flouncy in frilly dresses, the boys giddy in knee pants and sailor shirts. Standing silent and unnoticed by the bustling crowds were the shops below, the apartments above, the brownstones, the hotels, the theaters on Broadway and off, the monuments, the restaurants, the businesses, and, further along, the mansions and chateaux. Americans, far removed from the grim and desperate war scenes in Europe, continued with their daily routines as though nothing was different, nothing had changed, their lives not at all disrupted. If I hadn't heard the proclamations from the newsboys, I might not have known we were now a nation at war.

That afternoon, after I arrived home from work, my father showed me the newspaper article, his boyish, gap-toothed grin crooked as he read the words of those who made excuses for the war.

"The war is a warning against the past," he read, "against the aristocracy of Europe laying its hand on the enterprising society of a still-new America. Coercive governments, barbarianism, imperialism—these are the injustices against which Americans will fight. We have no aristocracy flourishing under the Stars and Stripes. There are no thousand-year-old castles across the purple mountains or the fruited plains, no royalty or very old blood. The newly birthed, bustling American cities aren't as ancient and elegant as they are in Europe. And now our American soldiers will help the Europeans do what they have been unable to do for themselves—end this war on the side of democracy."

My father slapped the newspaper onto the dining room table. "They don't see," he said. He sipped his coffee as he considered his words. "Everyone in Europe is a soldier now in one way or another. Their heroes are suffering from the new chemical weapons. They're suffering from the first bombardments from the airplanes above onto the men below. There are genocides and rebellions, but no one reports them, and the people here don't see them. They don't understand. Too many Americans already believe this is a war leading to something greater than itself."

"The Patriotism," I said.

"And it's spreading faster than a wildfire."

Three weeks later crowds swarmed the Manhattan streets for the "Wake up, America!" parade. Sparks from the Elevated trains were whisked up and away by morning breezes from the bay and hovered overhead like fireflies. People hustled and bustled, pushed and shoved, walked and talked, zigged and zagged around the automobiles following elliptical mazes around the city.

The morning of the parade was late April, the first trace of real spring, and I watched as the sun disappeared behind the high-rises leaving the skyline a haze of iridescent blue. I pulled my straw hat over my eyes and tried to keep within my own space so I wouldn't feel trapped in the crowd and overwhelmed by my claustrophobia. To help myself overcome the too-closeness I felt, I eavesdropped on snippets of passing conversations. People were sanguine in their praise of Wilson and the war.

Every school in New York City was closed that day so the children could exult in the miracle that is democracy. Suddenly, hundreds of people sounded their collective glee as a pretty girl in riding breeches galloped on horseback down Broadway.

"She looks misplaced," I said aloud, to no one in particular. "She looks like a country girl who's confused and lost her way down the city streets."

An older bystander wearing pinstripes and a derby leaned in my direction.

"She's meant to represent the spirit of Paul Revere when he alerted the American countryside to the approach of the British armies," he said.

"And why do we need to be alerted today?" I asked.

"Why," replied the gentleman, "she's alerting us to the peril of the Germans and their quest for world domination. She's meant to inspire us to believe in our strength as Americans and the need to use that strength to assure democracy in the new world order."

"There's all that to be found in the sight of a girl in breeches riding a horse through the city?" I asked. The gentleman found me facetious and didn't reply. He turned back to the parade to make meanings of his own without the distraction of frivolous questions from a young woman alone in a crowd.

I sighed as the parade featured countless riders on countless horsebacks with countless symbolic messages my too-literal mind couldn't grasp. There were marching bands aplenty alongside slim, apple-pie boys in their military garb, all walking beneath a great electric sign flashing: Absolute and Unqualified Loyalty to Our Country. People cheered when they saw it. Everyone, the shorter ones standing on their toes with their necks craned, the taller ones holding young children on their shoulders, the older men leaning on walking sticks, the women peeking demurely from beneath their parasols, and those leaning out the windows overhead, accepted the words as law. The 100% American message was even in the leaflets dropped onto our heads from the high-rises.

The 60,000 schoolchildren attending the spectacle waved American flags as they swayed to the beat of Sousa tunes and watched airplanes dive in and around the sky as though Newton's law of gravity need not apply to them. Besides the armed forces, representatives from the Red Cross marched, encouraging the women of America to volunteer to fight the nurse's fight. The Boy Scouts, the Salvation Army, the YMCA, the YWCA, and the Citizens National Defense League also marched, the latter group was created to bring attention to the fact that many police could be drafted, leaving New York City without lawful protection, corrupt as the Tammany Hall protection already was.

When I had seen enough I weaved myself back through the obstacle course of the crowd. The parade reminded me of the time I saw Houdini perform his escape act and I was disappointed because I couldn't believe the illusion. Others in the audience gasped and jumped from their seats whenever Houdini appeared before their eyes. They believed his deceptions just as the parade spectators believed the illusion, the parade only one more stunt pulled with lights, mirrors, and contraptions. Only President Wilson's effects needed a larger stage.

The next day in the *New York Times* a poem degrading the Germans caught my attention:

They call on God, blaspheming, as they plunge their hands in gore;
They've butchered millions, millions, and they'd butcher millions more.

Next to Van Zile's poem was a drawing of a strong-looking Marine with the Stars and Stripes billowing around him. I searched the columns for some reference to the woman suffrage displays taking place before Wilson's White House gates, but there wasn't even one. There was no mention that New York might become, with Arkansas, one of the first states to grant American women the vote. There was a blurb about the prohibition amendment some temperance groups were trying to push through Congress, but that received a brief paragraph of a mention. How often issues concerning women were relegated to the back pages, if they were referred to at all?

I walked to school the next morning with a vague dread of what I would find when I got there, afraid that the Patriotism had infected everyone everywhere beyond reason. The schoolhouse where I taught first grade was a whitewashed building barely visible behind lumbering elm trees, and when I arrived it was bustling with children. Boys and girls ran across the grass, some playing ball, some chasing each other, some swinging from the wood swings, others sitting and talking. I watched the laughing children and smiled. Here is what is real, I thought. Here is joy. I taught at a privately owned facility that brought only the richest children and their richer parents who wouldn't dare for their darlings to attend a school known merely as P.S. with an ordinary number attached to it. There was no prestige in attending public school, no prestige in doing something anyone else, provided they were young enough, could do.

"Mrs. Scofield is here!" cried one of my students. He ran to me and hugged my legs.

"Good morning, Andy," I said. "How are you today?"

"I'm fine, Mrs. Scofield."

Mrs. Miller stopped beside us and looked at Andy over her round spectacles, her expression severe. "Young man, she is not Mrs. Scofield. She is unmarried. She is Miss Scofield."

Andy shrugged and said, "Yes, ma'am," as was expected of him, and he ran away to play with his friends. Most of my students called me Mrs. Scofield, and I never corrected them. I thought they should have their time before they had to understand such things.

When class began that morning I saw how much the war was on their minds.

"What is war, Miss Scofield?"

"Mrs. Scofield, if soldiers are going across the ocean, will my daddy go too?"

"How do they know who to shoot?"

"Why are we fighting Germans? My grandmother is German, and she'd never shoot anyone."

"You see," I said, "in this case some leaders in Europe are choosing to use their guns and their airplanes to settle their problems. It seems they've forgotten what first graders know so well— to use their words."

"Do unto others as you would have others do unto you," said a little voice from the back of the room.

"Well put, Roger," I said.

"That's the Golden Rule," Roger said, squirming with delight. "I learned that from the Bible."

"I want you all to know," I said, "that when we vote, we have our say about who goes into public office and who stays there. If we don't like war, then we need to elect officials who don't like war. That is our right as American citizens."

"But women can't vote," said a little girl with gold ringlets and a starchily pressed dress. She shook her head and her ringlets bobbed.

"You're right, Clarissa, women can't vote. Here in New York women may receive the vote this year if all goes according to plan."

"I know that!" Clarissa squealed. "That's women's suffering!"

I began to correct her but stopped. Her label was more accurate than my own.

"My father said anyone against Wilson and the war is a traitor," said a freckled-faced boy named Stephen. "He says those people aren't real Americans."

"In this country we're free to express ourselves, even if our opinions are different from others," I said. "We have freedom of speech. You and I might have different opinions about the war, but neither one is right and neither one is wrong."

"But you can't be right because my father's always right. Besides, he says women can't vote because their brains are too small."

I let the subject drop with the silence. Whether the children were impressed at all, I couldn't tell from their glassy eyes. I took the morning's lesson from my desk and began writing out the vocabulary words from *McGuffey's First Reader* in white chalk on the blackboard. The children pulled the bulky textbooks from their school bags and opened to the page number I gave them. They followed with their fingers as they read.

See Tom skate. See Tom skate on the ice. See Tom skate on one foot on the ice.

"Doesn't Tom know it's spring?" asked a small voice.

"No," I said, "it seems he doesn't. Perhaps one of us should tell him."

The sun had finally broken through the gray-tinged clouds and the outdoors promised brightness away from the umbrella shade of the trees. It hardly seemed the day to be reading about poor boys in drab coats skating one-footed across the frozen pond. I closed the fable-ridden textbook that tried to teach morals based on ideals from long before. If I was bored looking at those flat words I could only imagine how the children felt.

"Here is your assignment," I said. "You will write Tom a letter explaining that it's spring and he doesn't need his ice skates and his sweater any longer. Think about the colors of spring. Think about the singing birds. Think about the warming rays of the sun and the flowers in bloom. Describe them to Tom. Since you can't ice skate in spring, what can you do in spring that you can't do in winter? Make spring sound wonderful for him, make it come alive so he'll be happy about putting his skates away until winter comes again. Raise your hand if you have an idea about something wonderful that happens in spring. Yes, Jasper?"

"The New York Giants start in spring."

"Yes, baseball starts in spring. What else? Emily?"

"Gardens grow in spring."

"Good. What else?"

"War starts in spring."

The children nodded together.

"Yes," I said. "This year war starts in spring."

Soon the children were scribbling away in their first-grade language, searching through the window for signs of spring to make real to Tom, their daydreamy friend who didn't see the sun outside. It was best to allow them time to think for themselves without throwing ideas and delusions at them. They would form their delusions soon enough.

When the dismissal bell rang the children were slower than usual to grab their books and skedaddle to the door. I followed behind them, straightening up as they left. There were chalk-boards to erase, books to align in order from tallest to shortest, blocks to arrange in symmetrical lines, artwork to hang on the walls, papers to file, and assignments for the following day to set in place. Then, as I left my classroom I felt the warmth of the children dissipate into stagnant silence and frustrated smiles. I walked the short corridor to the large, airless office by the front door. Sitting there, high and majestic on a gold-cushioned Chippendale chair, was Mrs. Rittenhouse, a thick-set, smileless woman who wore her heavy graying hair pulled into the traditional schoolmarm bun, lest anyone forget her role as the proprietor of the school. I breathed in deeply and approached the grand dame.

"Mrs. Rittenhouse," I said. She continued writing in her ledger, oblivious to me, so I stepped closer to her overlarge desk, feeling like a five-year-old trying to reach a kitchen cabinet where the sweets were hidden. "Mrs. Rittenhouse," I said again, louder this time. She condescended a nod in my general direction.

"Hello, Miss Scofield. How are we today?"

"I'm well, Mrs. Rittenhouse, thank you. I was wondering when the new supplies were expected. I still need chalk so the children and I can write on our blackboards, and I need..."

Mrs. Rittenhouse bared her teeth in her most complacent smile. "Whatever happened to the supplies I gave you at Christmas?" Her voice was syrupy sweet.

"It's April," I said.

There was hardly enough space for me in the office since Mrs. Rittenhouse's new desk of heavy, carved mahogany was so large it took up half the room. She saw me studying her prized piece of furniture and she patted it proudly.

"Beautiful, isn't it? Mr. Rittenhouse purchased it wholesale."

I ran my hand over the carved floral trim. "It's lovely," I said. "I'm wondering, though, since we're short of supplies so often..."

"It's a matter of appearances, Miss Scofield. I know how the teachers like to complain there aren't enough supplies or snacks for the children, but if the parents don't have a positive reaction as soon as they walk into the school then they won't enroll their children. If they don't enroll their children then there won't be any money for the school. And if there's no money for the school, well, I don't care so much for myself." She pulled herself upright, her face softening into pious demurity, her eyes downcast. "I'm a simple woman who lives simply, but what about the teachers? There wouldn't be money for your salaries. And what about the children? We must always consider the children. The children always come first at Rittenhouse Academy, and it isn't good for them to have such nonsense as teachers worrying about money."

The office was dim, even reticent as horizontal streams of sunlight peered through the drawn Venetian blinds. Suddenly, the front bell rang and two potential parents, a well-tailored husband and his bejeweled wife, walked in and stopped short at the sight of the overlarge desk that prevented them from going any further. The parents introduced themselves and explained their business —to enroll their little boy in the kindergarten class. Mrs. Rittenhouse offered them the grand tour of the school. She pointed out the paintings from the children hanging behind her desk with the artists' names in large, crooked letters. Beaming like a proud parent, she proclaimed, with a humble smile, "Oh, but the children will paint these beautiful pictures for me. Isn't it charming how children will attach themselves to me?" The parents, seeing the proof for themselves in the paintings, looked around that much more closely because here was a woman who understood the business of children.

When the parents turned away to inspect the artwork on the wall, Mrs. Rittenhouse opened the windows and shades to let in the sunshine that added an extra sparkle to the children's pearl-like smiles.

"Miss Scofield here teaches first grade," she told the parents, and they too condescended a nod in my direction. "Miss Scofield, why don't you tell Miss Eberhardt the Andersons will be coming to meet her."

Hilde Eberhardt was the kindergarten teacher at the school, and she was also my friend. When I walked into her classroom I saw her back door open. Outside Hilde sat under a tree with one of her tiny students in her arms, rocking the girl as the child's mother should have been rocking her, brushing some fallen strands of gold-brown hair from tear-filled eyes.

"It is all right, dear heart," Hilde said. "Your mamma, she will be here soon." Suddenly, a long black car pulled up and a well-dressed, Fifth Avenue-looking woman rushed from the car after her chauffeur opened her door. The woman grabbed the weeping girl from Hilde's arms.

"My precious!" the mother cried. "I lost track of time while I was shopping, but don't you worry, darling. Mother bought you a little blue dress you're going to die for!" Without a thank you for waiting with her child, the mother and her child disappeared into the car that disappeared down the road. Hilde sighed.

"Does she do that every day?" I asked.

"Every day. And every day Rachel cries while she waits."

Mrs. Rittenhouse opened the door to Hilde's classroom and showed the Andersons around. "Here's another one for you," I whispered. "Fresh bait for Mrs. Rittenhouse."

Hilde joined them in the classroom. At Mrs. Rittenhouse's request, Hilde explained the curriculum, the music program, and the art projects, speaking with the gentle patience I loved her for. Mrs. Anderson, tugging on the double strand of pearls decorating her collarbone, looked Hilde up and down in a different way than Mr. Anderson.

"Are you German?" Mrs. Anderson asked.

Hilde shook her head. "I'm a citizen here."

"But you're German."

"I am American."

Mrs. Anderson looked at her husband, who only had eyes for Hilde. "She's German," Mrs. Anderson said.

Mr. Anderson smiled. "I see."

Mrs. Anderson took her husband's arm and led him toward the door. "Thank you for your time, Mrs. Rittenhouse. We have several other schools we're looking into for our Johnny. He's highly intelligent, you see, and he needs to be challenged. I'm sure you understand."

Mrs. Rittenhouse smiled. "I'm certain after you've visited the other schools you'll see we have the most challenging program available for kindergarteners today. Isn't that right, Miss Eberhardt? Some parents have said their five-year-olds are ready for college after a year in this class."

Mrs. Anderson managed a curt nod before dragging her husband out of Hilde's classroom. With the Andersons safely away, Mrs. Rittenhouse's understanding smile dropped to a sneer directed at Hilde. Mrs. Rittenhouse said nothing as she removed herself to her office, probably to fume over the fact that her expensive new desk hadn't closed the deal with the Andersons.

Hilde shrugged as Mrs. Rittenhouse disappeared. Then she turned to me and smiled. "Come home with me, Rose," she said. "Mamma wants to see you."

I spent hours that afternoon sitting in the dining alcove in the Eberhardt's apartment overlooking the East River, listening to the family switch between English for my benefit and German for Hilde's 91-year-old grandfather. Mrs. Eberhardt bustled around the tiny kitchen, cooking enough to feed everyone in the building, laughing at a funny story about her girlhood in Stuttgart. There were times when, looking at the stout little woman with her wide smile, her bun-pulled hair, and her apron, I thought, so this is what a mother is. Grandfather Rumann sat in his rocking chair in front of the window and watched the city scenes below him. He was an elderly man who was forward-bent but up-looking, kind and grandfatherly toward anyone under the age of 70. But that afternoon, after the announcement of the new war, Grandfather Rumann looked sad, broken. I watched him while he stared out the window, his grief infecting me somehow. Hilde leaned close to me and whispered.

"Since the news of the war he's taken to his bed a lot," she said. "He's pained by the anti-German propaganda sweeping the city."

"You shouldn't tell him what happened today then," I said.

Mrs. Eberhardt stopped clearing the plates from the table. "What happened today?"

"It is nothing, Mamma," Hilde said. "Really, nothing."

Mrs. Eberhardt nodded, though the way she watched her daughter said she wasn't convinced. She glanced at her father sitting by the window and shook her head.

"My father, Hilde's grandfather, was walking around today and saw the new posters," Mrs. Eberhardt said. "They made him sad because it means the war is here now."

"Which posters, Mamma?"

"The Uncle Sams."

I had seen the eyesores myself plastered around town, the simple message meant to infect everyone with the Patriotism—a picture of a thin-faced, severe-looking, gray-haired man wearing the Stars and Stripes. "I Want You!" the poster read as Uncle Sam's menacing finger pointed at the young men of America, beckoning them to fight the brave fight.

Suddenly, Grandfather Rumann turned toward us, his eyes drooping, his face long.

"My two countries are at war when they don't need to be," he said in his halting English. He nodded in confirmation of his own words. "It is true. I am sad."

I nodded in commiseration. I didn't know how to tell him that I felt his ache within myself.

CHAPTER 4

$\mathcal{M}$y father and I attended many fundraisers in those new war days, not because he cared to donate to the Patriotism, but because he wanted to understand those who did. That warm, mid-May night, with the faintest humidity hanging like a canopy over the waterways, I walked into the ball-room at the Waldorf-Astoria to a confusion of red, white, and blue while the people, of those who weren't waltzing across the polished floor, spoke in determined tones about the necessity for loyalty to our country. The dinner was unremarkable, the wines watered, the conversations dull. The men were well-pressed and well-groomed, the women uncomfortable in their profusion of jewels and furs in spring. The women took pride in their chari-table works, though I often thought their charitable works were an excuse for throwing parties. Instead of calling it a ball, they called it a benefit for the war effort and no one was the wiser.

My father and I stayed close to each other until after dinner when he joined the men in the smoking room hoping to discover some new information that might shed some light on war-time subjects he found increasingly perplexing. Occasionally, I joined my father with the men, which caused some odd stares, though in many ways I felt more comfortable with the men. In the smoking room, the men looked similar to each other in their matching suits, their matching jeweled stickpins, and their matching chains across their matching waistcoats. They had similar mannerisms, with similar small smiles and similar tight nods. They encircled each other and laughed loudly and threw their hands on each other's shoulders and tried to best each other with their verbal wit. Unlike the men who looked the same but spoke as individuals, the women spoke the same but looked as unique as possible. I laughed whenever I saw a woman arrive at a social function in a dress remotely similar to a dress worn by another woman while both of the grand dames spent the night pouting.

Where the men congregated together in brotherhood, the women stood apart from each other, eyeing each other, deciding whether this woman was better dressed or prettier than she, had more expensive jewels or furs, had a man with better status or more wealth than hers. The men talked lightly about important matters. The women spoke seriously about nothing. The men had their accomplishments to make themselves known in the world. The women had their husbands. When a man felt another had bested him, he made a joke, bowed, and conceded his argument— usually. When a woman felt another had bested her she became a cat in attack position, back against the wall, tail up, claws out, figurative claws that scratched with pointed words.

I felt the scratch of the claws, more painful than the occasional leers I had to face when I joined my father with the men, and which my father stopped as quickly as they began with a cutting look, or which I stopped with cutting words. Listening to my father discuss Wilson's war efforts with a gray-bearded man already infected with the Patriotism grew tiresome, so I glanced in the mirrors that lined the walls, checked that everything was in place, and walked with my straightest bearing into a battlefield men can never understand.

Mrs. Rittenhouse was in the ballroom speaking with other

women of similar haughty disposition. I stopped near the door, trying to avoid Mrs. Rittenhouse's gaze, hoping to see a friendly face. Instead, I found myself next to an expensive-looking, bejeweled woman, perhaps in her fifties, wearing a lace and tulle gown with flounces of flowers that matched her silvering hair. She was the center of a conversation that no longer interested her, and she gestured toward me.

"You are Miss Scofield?" the woman asked. "My son Montgomery is under your father's tutelage at the *Times*. Your father is a man of integrity, even if he is liberal in his ideas. But he means well, and allowances must be made for those who mean well. I am Mrs. Carter."

"Mrs. Carter," said a younger woman, wide-looking in her barrel-line gown, "everyone knows who you are."

Mrs. Carter turned toward the speaker. "This young woman does not!" The wide-looking woman backed into the nosy bodies who wanted to hear everything to rehash at a later time.

"Montgomery said you're with the suffrage movement," Mrs. Carter said.

"I work closely with Mrs. Belmont," I said. "We hope to have the vote for women in New York this year."

Mrs. Carter clucked her tongue. She stepped closer to me and squinted. "So you're not involved with those militant women in Washington? Very good." She turned to one of the women closest to her. "We are very much against the suffrage movement, Mrs. Stewart, are we not?"

"We are, Mrs. Carter," said Mrs. Stewart.

"I'm sure Montgomery must have told you, Miss Scofield, that we're active members of the anti-suffrage campaign. We find the suffragettes to be wasting their time. They might as well wear trousers. They are unwomanly, and they are unsexed."

The surrounding women giggled. With a sharp look, Mrs. Carter silenced them.

"Do you support the prohibition amendment going through

Congress?" Mrs. Carter asked. "We are involved in the temperance movement. After we have the drink abolished we'll turn our attention to the moving pictures, which put immoral thoughts into young people's minds. Women must remember we are the upholders of morality. It's a duty we cannot take lightly."

"I enjoy the moving pictures and I go as frequently as I can," I said. "I don't recall any immoral thoughts put into my mind from them. I think the problems of society go deeper than liquor or moving pictures can account for."

Mrs. Carter clucked her tongue again, studying me as though I were a unique scientific specimen on display at a museum. "You are a nearly impudent young woman." She walked around me, side, back, side, front again, looking at me through the monocle on a long gold chain around her neck. I felt like a statue being appraised for auction. "Of course, you've planted your victory garden. Our European allies need food to eat since Germany is blocking their coasts, and we're going to lose many of our farmers as they become soldiers. We must do our duty and grow our own vegetables."

I had seen the posters around the city declaring: Hoe Behind the Flag—Plant a Victory Garden! I had seen neighbors tearing flowers and bushes from the dirt by their roots, tossing them aside to make room for family-sized crops of carrots, corn, peas, and turnips. Apartment dwellers rented vacant lots and subdivided them into individual gardens. There were articles in *Vogue* and *Good Housekeeping* declaring khaki a smart color for women and girls: Wear Khaki for Garden, Camp, Play or Drill.

"I haven't planted a victory garden," I said. "I haven't had the heart to pull out the flowers my aunt has worked so hard to tend for a cause I'm not sure I support."

Mrs. Carter dropped her monocle. "How old are you again? Montgomery has told me, but I can't recall."

"I'm 27," I said.

"You haven't much time," Mrs. Carter said. "Haven't you any other prospects?"

"Other prospects?"

"Yes, other prospects. Other men."

"I currently have no prospects."

"Why not? You're attractive and youngish."

"I haven't found a man I wish to marry."

"My dear, there aren't any men one wishes to marry. You choose one from the bunch and make the best of him you can."

"I would first like to make the best of myself."

"You certainly have modern ideas." She clucked her tongue yet again. "I've forgotten what Montgomery had to say about your mother. What does she think of your modern ideas?"

A woman standing behind Mrs. Carter whispered loudly enough for me to hear, "Her mother has been dead since she was a child."

Mrs. Carter nodded. "That explains it. The poor girl doesn't know any better." She thought a moment, then added, "I recall your aunt, Mrs. Wilcox. She and I met at a benefit for the Red Cross. I wonder why she didn't take it upon herself to teach you."

"To teach me what?" I said.

Mrs. Carter shook her head. She turned away as if I were no longer there. Mrs. Rittenhouse beckoned her, presumably to learn what we had been talking about. Suddenly, Mrs. Carter turned to me and said, "Since my son is so insistent we must see what can be done. You will come to tea this Thursday afternoon. My car will come for you at 3:40 p.m., and tea will begin at 4:00 p.m. precisely."

She walked away with Mrs. Rittenhouse, and I was left with engine-hot steam in my breath, wanting to shake down the ballroom with the weight of my aggravation. There is nothing wrong with me, I wanted to scream. I'm not ill. I'm not bored. I'm not biding my time. I want to live on my own terms. I won't be enchained. But these women wouldn't have understood, so I returned to the men's smoking room by my father's side and watched the red, white, and blue crepe paper jangle in the breeze of the ceiling fans. I felt as if I, too, were dangling from the ceiling while the other guests watched me jiggle and fidget for their entertainment.

Later that night, back at the brownstone, I wandered outside under the canopy of city-strewn stars to the small backyard where Cynthia tended our little plot of a garden. The anger from Mrs. Carter's presumptions still steamed my clammy brain, and I felt like my head was a pressure cooker ready to explode into messy shapes on the wall. If Mrs. Carter thought I was a nearly impudent young woman, then so be it. Watching the blooming, blushing rose bushes, marveling at the May-time burst of coral, purple, and magenta in the azaleas and rhododendrons reaching toward the hanging leaves of our sweet gum tree, I knew I couldn't tear out the flowers to make room for the vegetables others expected me to grow. This was one victory I wouldn't share in. I didn't have Cynthia's passion for gardening, but I wouldn't be shamed into using my personal space in a way others would have me. Standing in the backyard, pulling my shawl closer around my shoulders as the nighttime breeze blew cold, I decided I wouldn't plant a victory garden, not at all. Instead, I'd help Cynthia with the gardening. I'd help her plant as many flowers as our small patch of earth would hold, if only because I felt like I was being dared to.

But what about visiting Mrs. Carter on Thursday afternoon at 4 p.m. precisely? I wasn't going. Why should I? She was as cold and haughty as her son. She seemed to think I ought to shrivel up and die an old maid any day now. Besides, she thought I was a nearly impudent young woman. She couldn't remember a thing Montgomery told her about me, though apparently he shared our whole evening with her.

And yet, I was curious. What could she want with me? What

did she want to teach me, and, more importantly, what did she think I needed to learn? Besides, she was sending her car for me, so I wouldn't have to make any effort to get there. And it might be my only chance to see what it looked like inside one of those mansions. Then the thought occurred to me that if I didn't go Mrs. Carter would think I was afraid, or weak, and I wouldn't give her the satisfaction. Even after much debating I hadn't made up my mind. I might go, or I might not. When I mentioned my possible Thursday afternoon plans to my father, he blanched. He put his coffee cup onto the end table, giving me his complete attention.

"What does Mrs. Carter want with you?" he asked.

"She invited me to tea."

"Is that all she wants?"

"That's what I want to find out."

"I don't know, Rose."

"She's sending her car for me. That's fancy, isn't it?"

"That's very fancy, but I still don't think you should go."

At that moment my father made up my mind for me. I was going to tea with the Carters. If I had been unsure before, his reluctance for me to go made me have to. I loved my father, and while I got my good qualities from him, I also got his stubborn-ness. As soon as anyone told me not to do something, even if that anyone was my father, I had to do it or risk feeling like they had the best of me, which I couldn't allow.

"What harm can come from it?" I said. "Mrs. Carter invited me. Her husband is on the board of directors of the paper. Maybe I need to say yes or you'll be fired."

My father pointed at me, his slate-gray eyes flashing. "Don't you dare say yes, Rose. No matter what any Carter ever says to you, don't you ever say yes."

"Even to tea?"

He studied his fingernails, his black shoe polish, the Victrola near the window, and the newspapers on the coffee table. "Will Montgomery be there?"

"Mrs. Carter didn't say," I said.

My father nodded distractedly as he stared out the window at a couple walking arm-in-arm across the quiet street.

I kissed his cheek. "Don't worry," I said. "I'm going to drink tea from some fine china with hand-painted periwinkles that cost more than either of us makes in a year. I'll have a look around, I'll be satisfied that I went, and then I'll come home. I won't say yes to anything else."

"Do you promise?"

I laughed at the intensity behind my father's question. "I promise."

Thursday afternoon arrived and I prepared myself to sit through tea with the Fifth Avenue Carters. As I scanned my wardrobe for the right dress to wear (what does one wear to Fifth Avenue, I wondered?), I realized Mrs. Carter was correct about me in one sense: I was a nearly impudent young woman.

I had always been that way. I was raised by my father, and he, being a man, kept mostly the company of men. I knew what my father's friends were up to, even at the poker games behind the closed kitchen door when Mrs. Harris should have been minding me but had instead fallen asleep on the overstuffed settee under the window. As I passed the kitchen door I heard the remarks from my father's cronies: Hey! look at that broad here, or Wow! look at those ankles there. My wife nags too much and women nag too much and what do those dames know about anything and they want to vote and Wow! look how she fills out that dress and have I told you my wife nags too much? One morning I woke up appalled—I realized I was no different from the women I had heard leered at, sneered at, grinned at, squinted at, and complained of, and I feared that one day I, too, would be the topic of mean-spirited laughter and unfriendly words. I didn't want to be that woman.

In my childhood of traipsing energy and buoyant laughter, I ran about with abandon in the streets, my auburn hair falling and unrestrained, my clothes not constricting dresses but knickers and free. As I grew older, I understood that my young girlhood of running, jumping, singing, and laughing was the closest to self on earth I would ever know. The older I grew, the more constrained my life became.

When I was no longer a little girl, my father felt his sole influence was no longer enough for his blossoming Rose. His mourning wounds for his dead wife were slashed open afresh, as though 11 years hadn't passed and I was still a motherless baby girl. He called on his mother and sister for help, and they meant well, my grandmother and aunt. They did their best, but it was from them my confusion began.

While other girls played with dolls, practicing for motherhood, dreaming of husbands and babies though they hadn't the slightest idea about either, I knew what kind of woman I didn't want to be—one who was ogled, one who nagged, and one too dim-witted to vote. But my grandmother and my aunt, well-meaning though they were, tried to unlearn from me everything I knew, deep and astute though that knowledge was:

"Smile more."

"Don't run. It's not ladylike to run."

"Don't speak unless you're spoken to."

"Don't ask too many questions."

"Smile more."

"Don't spend so much time at the nickelodeons. They'll put ideas in your head."

"Don't frown. You'll make lines between your eyes."

"Smile more."

I did whatever I needed to do to keep the peace in my red-brown brownstone. I wore uncomfortable clothes with gloves and boater hats. I spent time with growing girls my age and listened to them talk about which boys to like and which to ignore and which new fashions from Paris were to die for and which color lipstick they would wear to get the boys to look their way if make-up weren't only for naughty women. When I didn't smile, for whatever reason, my grandmother would ask my father, "What's wrong with Rose?"

And my father would answer, "Maybe she doesn't feel like smiling today."

And my aunt would say, "But young ladies should always smile. It's our job to be polite and pleasant." And my grandmother would whisper, "Rose thinks too much, Martin." My father nodded and changed the subject.

My aunt Cynthia, my mother's sister, was different. When she moved back to New York after her husband died I found a new calm in my life. For the first time, I saw a different kind of woman, the kind I always knew must exist somewhere. She was herself at all times, and she did whatever was in her heart to do. She didn't ask permission or forgiveness. She spoke to men with the same serene dignity she spoke to women. If she wanted to help the suffrage movement, she did. If she wanted to plant flowers, she did. If she wanted to help my father research an article or type a clean copy of his column, she did. I wanted to do, too, and it was this can-do spirit Mrs. Carter found nearly impudent about me.

The stiffly dressed chauffeur arrived at the brownstone at 3:40 p.m. He said nothing when I answered the door. He said nothing as we walked to the curb where the long car stretched from one end of our block to the next. He said nothing as he drove the city streets, past corners, around slower moving vehicles and trolley cars. We arrived in front of a castle-like mansion along Fifth Avenue, one of a streetful of European-influenced dwellings that housed the wealthiest New York City could boast of. The chauffeur said nothing as he opened the door for me after he parked near the curb, and I was greeted by blank-faced servants who allowed me past the wrought-iron gate at the front of the property, through the straight-lined, emotionless garden, up the marble stoop toward the cedar wood fretwork where the double French doors with the gold fleur-de-lis knockers sat like guards to protect the family from intruders. The housekeeper opened the door, an old, humorless woman made more severe by the heaviness of the black and white livery she wore. She was nothing like Mrs. Harris, who found beauty in setting out dessert on rose-petal plates and who laughed to no end.

I was shown into the parlor, a lavishly furnished room with the same stark coldness as the rest of the house. There was nowhere to sink into like there was at the brownstone, where the overstuffed furniture invited loiterers to daydream. At the Carters' the chairs were Chippendale, upright and rigid, the tables small, leaving little room for family mementos. Even the sofa was thin with hardly room enough on the silk upholstery to sit back comfortably. Mrs. Carter appeared, back erect, hand out as though she were waiting for me to kiss her ring, or curtsey and back away, the Queen had arrived. She gestured for me to sit in the green silk wing chair across from where she sat on the green silk sofa. A nervous, skinny girl in black and white livery scurried in, carrying a silver tea tray. After she placed it on the long table the silverware clanked and clanged under her shaking hands. Mrs. Carter shooed her away.

"She is a ridiculous creature," Mrs. Carter said. "I took her on because I thought something could be made of her, but I was sadly mistaken."

I was already sorry I was there, and I wondered how quickly I could excuse myself. I had come because I was curious. I always wondered what it was like inside the Fifth Avenue mansions, alongside J. Pierpont Morgan and the wealthy elite. This was my chance to see the luxury many hold as their highest aspiration for this life. But I wasn't impressed. I didn't care for the costly price tags that were removed long ago but were evident everywhere. We are expensive, the decor shouted. You cannot afford us. I didn't care for the flat-faced servants. I didn't care for the ostentatious furnishings that were uncomfortable and aloof. I wasn't impressed with this house that wasn't a home but a museum. I wanted to return to my small, comfortable red-brown brownstone that wasn't nearly as fashionable, but it was overstuffed and snug. But the Carters' servants had prepared tea for me, so I would be polite for as long as I could, then make my excuses and leave.

Mrs. Carter was an expert at small talk, as one of her social position needed to be. She discussed with great interest the warmer weather, the signs of summer in the bluebirds flying above the flowering trees at Central Park or the crowds frequenting the seashore. Soon two young women, Mrs. Carter's daughters, Amy and Sybil, both pale, withdrawn, and looking largely unwell, joined us. I was introduced to them, and they feigned a nod as they eyed me curiously and sat with their necks straining toward the ceiling like giraffes reaching for foliage on a tree.

"My husband won't come," said Mrs. Carter. "He is detained with more important matters. Montgomery wanted to be here, but your father had business for him at the office."

"I see," I said.

The housekeeper returned with a pushcart filled with teatime treats like vanilla cream cake and buttery madeleines. She served us on iridescent bone china plates that were so delicate they looked like paper-thin sheets of mother-of-pearl. She poured the tea into iridescent bone china cups I could see my fingers through. I would have to tell my father I was right—the china looked like it cost more than our yearly salaries combined. As I stirred milk into my tea with a silver spoon, Mrs. Carter shook her head and clucked her tongue.

"Miss Scofield, one does not stir one's beverage so others can hear. One stirs silently without touching spoon to rim."

She then instructed me about which was the salad fork, where the knife goes in a table setting, and how to fold one's napkin on one's lap. I found her lecture amusing and laughed aloud. When she looked at me with all seriousness, I lowered my eyes and stirred my tea in a caricature of demurity. That pleased the Fifth Avenue Carters very much, and they didn't notice my near impudence.

"Her posture, Mother," said Amy, the youngest daughter.

"Miss Scofield, do pull your shoulders back," Mrs. Carter said.

"Mrs. Carter," I said, "I'm sure you didn't invite me here for etiquette lessons."

"Why else should I invite you?"

"I thought it was an act of hospitality because my father has taken your son under his wing."

Mrs. Carter nodded. "This is all about my son."

"She doesn't understand, Mother," said Sybil, watching me over the teacup she held too high.

"She will learn," Mrs. Carter said.

She clucked her tongue once more, and she looked at me as if deciding which wallpaper to use in the foyer. The housekeeper arrived to clear away the plates, the cups, and the silverware, and suddenly the room was spotless, as if I had never been there, all evidence of my presence swept aside. The electric broom was brought in. I took this as my cue to leave, though I wasn't able to escape before receiving an invitation to accompany the Carter ladies downtown to a temperance meeting the following evening, which I politely declined.

Hilde convinced me to go to the temperance meeting. She wanted to hear for herself about the temperance platform. Her father had been a heavy drinker and it caused much suffering in her family, even after his death.

"Perhaps if alcoholic beverages were taken away, even for a

little while, then people would take the money they were using to acquire drink and use it for their families."

"It's an idealistic goal," I said. "But it will never work. As soon as you tell someone he can't have something, he wants it even more."

As Hilde and I walked the busy blocks to the temperance meeting we came across an office where men in their calf-length overcoats gathered to look at the posters hanging in the window. The sign above the door read "Headquarters National Association Opposed to Woman Suffrage." Hilde and I glanced inside and saw women much like Mrs. Carter and Mrs. Rittenhouse, women who thought they were moral but were only concerned about morality as it suited them. Whether the men agreed or disagreed with the propaganda displayed in the window, literature about how women's brains are smaller and their physiology won't allow them to exert themselves in such a way that would allow them to be proper voters, about how the entry of women into public life would bring disaster to American society, it was impossible to tell by their impassive faces.

"How can women be against women voting?" Hilde asked.

"The women in the anti-suffrage campaign believe the family is the center of society," I said. "They believe if authority in the family is divided, then there will be social anarchy. It's not that they believe women don't have power, but they believe women's power is in the domestic realm where they can put to good use their conjugal and motherly virtues. They say that to keep a well-tended home and raise productive members of society, that's the highest privilege of womanhood."

"They're not wrong," Hilde said. "Being a good mother is the most important job there is."

"Those of us fighting for woman suffrage want women to have choices, that's all. The vote is the first step in guaranteeing those choices, but the Antis don't see it that way. Of course, the hypocrisy of their actions hasn't occurred to them. While they say women are too frail for the arduous task of managing political campaigns, they're waging a political campaign by lobbying extensively in Washington."

"I heard more women are working against the suffrage amendment than there are working for it," Hilde said.

"It's true."

Inside the temperance meeting were too many well-dressed, bejeweled women with feather-topped hats and stale perfume, too many loud voices proclaiming beliefs I didn't believe. To take my mind from the enclosure I felt as the women pressed around me, I fell into my usual claustrophobia cure, impolite enough to eavesdrop on the conversations around me. Closest to me was a group of wealthy-dressed women discussing the "domestics situation."

"There aren't enough good ones to go around," said a young red-haired woman. "You're so lucky, Virginia, to have one who works so hard. Mine works eight hours a day and all she ever finishes are the floors."

"I don't have to lift a finger," said Virginia, a well-rounded, flaxen-haired woman. "I drop my clothes on the floor and my girl is there to pick them up."

"How much do you pay her?" asked the red-haired woman.

"I don't know, dear. Thomas takes care of that."

"I pay my girl three dollars a week," said a dark-haired, severe-looking woman.

"Three dollars a week?" asked another.

"The other women who use her pay her two dollars but I pay three. She's not a live-in, and she works for other families. Besides, she's Irish and she's not educated. Three dollars a week is more than she'd get anywhere else."

Their conversation turned to who wore which fashions from Paris, who had gained the most weight, and where their next holidays would be. Mrs. Carter arrived, regal as always and surrounded by her court of fervent hangers-on. She gestured for me to sit beside her, and I introduced Mrs. Carter and her daughters to Hilde. Mrs. Carter clucked her tongue as she considered my friend through her monocle.

"Do you understand the importance of the temperance movement?" she asked Hilde. "We believe it is necessary to eradicate the evil liquid from the mouths of our men."

"I agree that the time and money spent on liquor could best be used in other ways," Hilde said.

"You are German," said Mrs. Carter.

"I am an American," Hilde said.

"You are from Germany?"

"Yes."

"We are very much against the Germans. Do you know what pains you people have caused decent Americans?"

I wanted to lead Hilde away from that ridiculous woman, but Hilde responded politely to Mrs. Carter and stayed stubbornly in her seat.

"I want to hear what the speakers have to say," Hilde said.

"But Hilde…"

"I will stay."

I stopped listening to the rhetoric that was only a rewording of the anti-suffrage platform. The temperance movement was simply another attempt to limit individual freedom and personal choice. After the speakers finished and coffee and cake were served, Mrs. Carter approached me.

"Certainly, this makes more sense than the suffrage movement, Miss Scofield. We'll expect you to write letters to Congress and make telephone calls Monday evening at 6 p.m. precisely. Next month we shall go to Washington to assist the anti-suffrage cause, and we'll expect you there, as well."

"I'm not helping the temperance movement," I said. "Making liquor illegal will only create a black market for it, and my belief in a woman's right to vote isn't negotiable."

"I told you, Mrs. Evenson," Mrs. Carter said to a bejeweled, older woman beside her. "She is nearly impudent, but she will learn."

"You're mistaken if you think I'm going to allow myself to be taught by you." I took Hilde's hand, and as we pushed our way past the gawking women I heard Mrs. Carter say, "You will learn, Miss Scofield."

I pretended I didn't hear and kept walking away.

CHAPTER 5

$\mathcal{A}$t school the following week I found Mr. and Mrs. Rittenhouse in the book room next to the shelves, their heads hanging over the open textbooks in their hands. On the floor by their feet was a mound of books, and Mr. Rittenhouse took the pile from the floor and threw the books into the nearby trashcan.

"They threw the German language textbooks into the trash," I told Hilde as we sat with our Coca-Colas in the soda shop across the street from school.

Hilde nodded. "They have already spoken to me. I am not to teach German any longer, and I am not to be heard speaking German near the children. Mrs. Rittenhouse said it is not good for the children to hear the language of American enemies."

"She's a fool."

"But if she is a fool then we are surrounded by fools because everywhere there are people who share her opinion."

Suddenly, from the back of the diner near the counter, came loud, raucous laughter. Hilde and I glanced in that direction, but the diner was crowded with the suppertime crowd and we saw nothing to interest us. Hilde put down the change for her soda and stood near the table. She tried to smile, but her sadness left a worried ring around her large blue eyes.

"Are you leaving already?" I asked.

"Excuse me, yes. I need to go home to see Grandfather. He wasn't well when I left this morning."

"Give him my love."

"I will." She hugged me close. "Thank you for being my friend, Rose."

"I should be thanking you, Hilde."

She pushed the diner door open and disappeared down the busy street. As I watched her leave I heard voices raised in a sentimental English song, one that spoke of leaving and longing:

Good-bye, Piccadilly,
Farewell, Leicester Square,
It's a long, long way to Tipperary,
But my heart's right there!

Everyone sat taller, listening. Then came another song, this one parade-like and marching in its up-tempo cadence. The lyrics had done more to help spread the Patriotism than any government propaganda. It was a simple tune with one-syllable lyrics, and its military-inspired melody was easy to sing. Written by Yankee Doodle Dandy himself, it was vaudeville star Nora Bayes, known as the Empress of the Two-a-Day, who first brought her audiences joyously to their feet as they, too, came to believe that this was a glorious war. In a matter of days the song was available in sheet music and on Victrola records. Everyone in the diner knew the words, and everyone sang. Even I couldn't help humming along:

Over there,
Over there,
Send the word,
Send the word over there...

There was a cheerfulness in the diner that comes with camaraderie in a crowd. When the song was done, those seated at the counter or in the booths resumed their conversations, but the lightness remained. Then from the back of the diner came loud words:

"Hey! You're the dame who slept through our whole act!"

I smiled at the young men headed in my direction. I should have recognized them as the ringleaders in the sing-a-long. The Bell Brothers squeezed themselves into my booth for two.

"Hello, boys," I said. "I hope my father was able to hold up his end of the bargain. Did his review get you onto the Big Time?"

The boys looked at each other and shrugged.

"Your old man did a great job," said Max. "Our own mother couldn't have written a better review for us, if she could write in English, that is. But no one in Albee's camp saw the column that day, or if they did they didn't care."

"I'm sorry," I said. "My father has been raving about your act ever since we saw you."

"You didn't see us," Adam said. "You were sleeping."

"I see you won't let me live that down."

"No, I won't. I was highly offended."

"Don't worry about us," Max said, leaning closer to me across the table. "We've been through this before. We have the summer to retool some bits and try them around town. Next season we won't let those big shots get away without seeing us." The boys nodded as if they had come to that decision before.

"Kitty," said Jacob, his shy smile lighting up as he reached for the blond waitress' hand, "will you marry me?"

"You got any dough?" Kitty asked. From the way her narrow eyes fixed on Jacob, she seemed to consider his offer.

"Dough? Who needs dough?"

"You need dough if you want to do any baking," Max said.

"We can live on love!" Jacob said.

"Not with you, chump." Kitty smiled coyly at Max, then sashayed, hips first, to the next table. Max understood.

"Looks like she wants to do some baking with you, Maxie," Adam said.

"I could make some cupcakes with a bird like that," Max said.

"You know," said Jacob, "I could use a beer."

"They don't sell beer here," David said.

"They won't be selling beer anywhere soon," said Adam. "Not if those tight old prohibition ladies have their way."

"I'm moving to Canada if it happens," said Max.

Looking at the brothers, I realized there were only four. "Where's Stuart?" I asked. Jacob made a gesture across his throat with his finger as if he were slicing bread. "Oh, no," I said.

"Worse than that," said Max. "He's married."

Adam nodded. "He got nervous when we had to register for the draft. He heard married men were let off so he married the first girl he tripped. He also heard farmers were let off, but he couldn't catch any cows. He's only good at chasing chickens. Max here is too old to be drafted."

"Yah," said Max. "I'm 32, already washed up as far as the government is concerned."

"Even if you weren't old," Adam said, "they still wouldn't take you since you're half-blind. Why else would you want to go out with that waitress later? Obviously, you can't see her."

I cleared my throat. "My father said it was so chaotic at the draft registration that the National Guard had to be called in," I said.

"True," said Jacob. "I saw it myself."

"There were a lot of fellows who hardly spoke English, which didn't help move things along," David said. "But it wasn't all that bad. Other than waiting in line all day all we had to do was fill out a card with our name, address, characteristics, occupation—we put Wandering Jews—and sign a statement saying we're willing to serve in the army, which we're not, but the guys who wouldn't sign were arrested so we signed. At least we can't be called slackers."

"Could you be drafted?" I asked.

"I suppose," said Adam. "I'm 29, so I'm not old like Max. I'm not married, so I'm not dead like Stuart. Jakey, Dave, and I have to report for medical exams. The three of us are probably fair game."

"Aren't you too young, David?" I asked.

"Nope. I'm 20, so I'm exactly right as far as the government's concerned."

"I thought you were younger than that," I said.

David nodded. "Everyone does."

The thought of the draft President Wilson had set in motion brought a damper over the high spirits of the brothers. Wilson had called for 600,000 volunteers to go across the pond, and every day young men happily signed on Uncle Sam's dotted line. Only moments before the brothers were singing "Over There" with such zest they prompted a crowd of strangers to join them. But the thought of actually going over there, to air-dropped bombs, to brain-drilling gases, to earth-dug trenches and best-friend or brother corpses sleeping beside them in the night, silenced the clamorous hurricanes. I said goodbye to the look-alike brothers and excused myself. It was too much lately, one problem after another with the war, the prejudice against Germans that hurt Hilde and her family, the Patriotism, the Rittenhouses, the Fifth Avenue Carters. I wanted to get away and be alone, and there was only one place that would settle me when I felt antsy that way.

I walked toward Times Square, watching the automobiles passing by, bulky, boxy masses with open tops and sunglassed drivers with scarves thrown stylishly around their necks, moving on their wheels wherever they wanted. I was 17 when Henry Ford created the Model-T with fewer parts than competitors used for their automobiles. As a result, Ford charged a good deal less for the Model T than the more expensive models, and suddenly a toy for the rich was accessible to everyone. When demand for the car exceeded Ford's ability to keep up, he initiated the factory assembly line where each worker had a specific, unskilled job to do in the manufacturing process. Suddenly, America was a nation on wheels, and as I walked I wished I had wheels too. I quickened my pace to the Rialto Theater, hoping to get there in time for the early evening show. As I bought my tickets I decided I would buy myself a Model T. It shouldn't be too hard to put away some savings from my salary each month until I had enough to purchase an automobile, I thought. I was envious of the passing cars, the drivers honking their horns, and I took comfort in my decision. With a car I could go anywhere I wanted—Maine, California, even Canada, the top of the world. I knew I would probably never travel farther than Washington to help Alice Paul and Lucy Burns push the national suffrage amendment through Congress, but the knowledge that I could drive myself anywhere in the country if I wanted was important because that meant real freedom to me.

The Rialto Theater was a moving picture palace that rivaled a European opera house with its embellished architecture. As I searched for a seat I realized that if I were looking to escape the Patriotism, the Rialto was the wrong place to go. Theaters had abandoned the neutrality policies that asked audiences not to voice opinions when war films played. The film industry had caught the Patriotism as well, and now audiences were encouraged to cheer for the heroic Allies and boo the barbarous German "Huns." Newsreels showed Total War where high-flying zeppelins drowned those below in pain-filled gas, adding new dimensions to wartime suffering. There were scenes of German submarines, U-boats, and tiny children in gas masks, scenes of a genocide in Turkey that would never be acknowledged—men, women, and children marched into the parched desert and left to starve and thirst to extinction. Propaganda pieces like *How I Can Best Serve My Country* were featured across the country, along with army recruiters present during the screenings to enroll the young men suddenly infected with the Patriotism. If the films didn't seal the deal, then the Four Minute Men, speakers who gave sermons between reels about why young men needed to enlist, why women needed to join the Red Cross, why everyone needed to plant their victory gardens, often did. If there were ideas to be put into the public psyche, the motion picture palaces were the places to do it. The theaters quickly became centers for American loyalty.

I found my way to my usual seat on the center balcony. I liked it better there than down front with everyone else crowded around you where you're packed in tight. From the top I had a better view, and there were times when I had the entire balcony to myself, which I preferred. I sat as the one-reel short flickered onscreen showing President Wilson, looking grim and grand-motherly in his owl-eyed glasses, dictating an extract of the war message to Congress and calling on us to buy war bonds. Then came the trailers with some of the most famous celebrities of the day doing their part to sell the bonds. Flash. Mary Pickford at a San Francisco rally where one million dollars was subscribed to the war effort. Flash. Charlie Chaplin and Douglas Fairbanks subscribed for $100,000 each, prompting their fans to subscribe. Flash. Pauline Frederick, Theda Bara, William S. Hart, and Ethel Barrymore appealed to the loyalty of the masses. Flash. Douglas Fairbanks sold $500,000 worth of bonds in New York before going on a cross-country train tour where he sold one million dollars worth by the time the train reached California. The messages from all the trailers were the same: Say YES to the war effort!

When the tinkering piano music began and the shadows glimmered before me, I was mesmerized. There were no other patrons in the balcony that late afternoon show, and with the theater lights out there was no one to look at, nothing to see except the sputtering images on the screen, figments of people, hints in shades of gray, living in another world from mine entirely, their words merely expressions or gestures. Their colorlessness made them surreal, abstract. The people onscreen didn't look tangible, their actions quick-time, too fast and jolt-like. Still, their problems, their loves, their dreams, and their quests were more colorful than any I knew in my quiet life. I was awed by the moving figures on the screen, and though I knew I couldn't reach out and touch them, I allowed myself to believe I could. There was an impression of depth where there was nothing but smooth, simulated movement. My imagination embellished it all.

That afternoon the film was *Inside the Lines*, about a British officer who masqueraded as a German spy masquerading as a British officer to foil the German plot to destroy the English fleet. I concentrated on the faces, and the gestures, and for the first time, I realized it was possible to have a voice without speaking. After the first two reels the black sign with white words appeared on the screen: Part One—Please Wait for Part Two. When the feature was over the audience came out of its collective trance. Some people spoke to their neighbors while others watched the newsreels of boys in fatigues carrying the dead from the trenches in a world that felt too far away.

One week later I saw a cartoon of "The Sinking of the Lusitania"—the reason why America joined this European war. The large ship sliding through the ocean alongside schools of fish fell into a dark gray as it was hit by a well-aimed missile and exploded to bits. The crowd jeered at the screen, shaking fists and grimacing, venting their frustrations at the audacity of those godless Huns.

As the Lusitania sank before my eyes, I saw a man climb the stairs to the balcony and sit a few rows away. Then he moved to the seat behind me.

"Hey! You're the dame who slept through our whole act!"

When he leaned closer I recognized his chestnut waves in the flickering light.

"Hello, Adam."

Adam climbed over the seat and sat beside me. There was something in the honesty of his smile, the friendliness, which put me at ease. "Here by yourself?" he asked, looking at the empty seats surrounding us.

"I like being by myself sometimes. I can do what I like without having to answer to anyone."

"I know what you mean. I had to sneak away to come here on my own without someone hanging on me."

"I thought you looked different. No brothers?"

"The Inseparables—that's what Pop calls us. Are they showing Chaplin today?"

"They showed Chaplin last week. Today is war movies, tomorrow is war movies, and the day after will be war movies."

"It's a good thing Chaplin is making a war movie or we'd never see him again. He's the best as far as I'm concerned."

"Fatty Arbuckle is a close second."

Adam nodded. "I knew I liked you. So what other war movies have you seen?"

"Saturday I saw *The Claw of the Hun*."

"What was that about?"

"A young man who tries to prove to his mother the extent of Hun espionage and the need to fight the enemy. His mother finally relents and allows him to enlist. Then last week I saw DeMille's *The Little American*."

"I haven't seen that yet, but I heard it's selling out wherever it plays. Mary Pickford is such a pixie, isn't she?"

I thought of her child-like curls and her little girl face and laughed. "Yes, she is a pixie."

"Is the story any good?"

"Pickford faces Germans in a chateau in France where the Kaiser's soldiers line up French peasants and shoot them for the fun of it. Pickford tries to phone for help, but she's found and sentenced to be shot."

"Let me guess. She lives."

"She does. She's saved by French shellings on the chateau. She escapes and falls exhausted beneath a cross in a destroyed church."

"The cross in the church is a nice touch."

"You can't escape the Patriotism even at the moving pictures these days."

"The what?"

The title of the second feature, *Daughter Angela*, flashed on the screen. "Never mind," I said.

Daughter Angela was a five-reel story, something about an old man's granddaughter who uncovers the enemy activities of the housekeeper's son and outwits the efforts of the spies, which ended with rousing applause from the 100% American audience in the Rialto. Instead of watching the film I watched Adam Bell. He was far more entertaining. His smile lit like joy behind his verdigris eyes during the lighter moments, he grimaced at the harder parts, and he applauded at the end like the others. His face was so changeable, the way his expressions flowed from one emotion to the next, so different from other men I knew who held themselves flat and wouldn't show great feeling in any direction. If Adam wanted to burst out laughing because something on the screen tickled him, he did. If he wanted to clap because he liked it when the bad guy got it in the end, he did. At one point, he was so engrossed in the drama he grabbed my hand and squeezed until the tension in the scene passed.

After the final film was over I stood to leave and Adam helped me with my shawl. Then he offered his arm. We lingered, waiting for the crowd on the floor to clear away. When we neared the door, Adam eyed the straw-hatted, arm-banded piano player, watching the pianist's fingers as they stumbled across the ivory keys, though the pianist didn't notice, being too wrapped up in watching his fingers himself.

"That's not how you play that song," Adam said. "He's not using the pedals right."

Adam went to the upright piano and smiled at the pianist, making an instant friend. He said, "Now if you use the pedals like this," he put his foot down, "and if you play in this key," he put his fingers on the keyboard, "the song will sound better."

Adam played the same tune the pianist had been playing, only now there was a roundness to the melody that wasn't there before. The pianist was just a boy, maybe 16 years old, and he looked thrilled at this new knowledge. Adam held his arm out to me and we left the theater, the pianist still waving thanks to Adam.

"That was nice of you to help that boy," I said.

"He looked like a nice kid, and he reminded me of myself when I was his age. I think I knew maybe three songs on the piano, all in one key, and I was playing in a nickelodeon. I played at four or five of them. I got canned from every one. But that's enough about me. Tell me about you."

"I'm a schoolteacher," I said.

Adam's eyes bulged, his cheeks puffed, and he looked as if he swallowed boiling lava. "Sorry," he said. "I had some unfortunate experiences in school and the word teacher brings back some tough memories. You don't look like a teacher."

"I teach first grade."

"If my first grade teacher looked like you I would've stuck around even longer than I did. Do you like teaching?"

"I love the children."

"I bet they love you too. They're lucky to have you as their teacher."

"Thank you," I said.

"What do you do when you're not teaching?"

"I volunteer with the woman suffrage movement."

"I read in the paper that the women in New York will most likely get the vote this year. Seems the Tammany bigwigs are going to back the women since they don't want to offend future voters."

I nodded, pleased he knew what was happening in the movement. "Right now it looks good for us," I said.

"What will you do if the vote goes through in the fall?"

"I'll continue teaching, and then I'll go to Washington to help the national movement as often as I can." I looked into Adam's verdigris eyes and asked, "Have you been called for your physical yet?"

"I don't have to worry about being drafted, and neither does David. Jakey is the only one who might get called for duty."

"Has he been told to report yet?"

"Not yet."

He became thoughtful as we passed the people on the sidewalk and the cars in the streets. Suddenly, for a reason I didn't understand, the city seemed to fall in on itself. The sense of collapse must have come from the sun fading in the west, leaving the skyscrapers in close-knit shadows that covered everything. The mass of people pushed themselves forward without looking left or right, and I felt my claustrophobia pressing me down. Outside in the open air I couldn't breathe. I thought the whole cityscape was staring at me, closing me in, pushing me somewhere I didn't want to go. I watched the skyscrapers, waiting for them to crash to the ground. I slipped over a crack in the sidewalk and stumbled. Adam put his arms around my waist to keep me on my feet.

"Are you all right?" he asked.

"I tripped," I said, embarrassed by my imaginary frights.

"Did you know you can get paid to trip? I trip all over the stage during our shows. It gets some good laughs, and I've twisted my ankle only once or twice. Now you can take a trip, but then you have to know where you're going. I don't usually know where we're going. That's Max's department."

I wondered if Adam could see the gratitude in my eyes. We continued walking, only now we were holding hands.

"Tell me more about yourself, Rose."

"I don't want to bore you."

"I'm not bored. Tell me."

"What do you want to know?"

"What else do you do when you're not teaching besides work for the suffrage movement and spend every spare moment at the Rialto?"

"I'm helping my aunt tend the small garden in our backyard."

"Growing a victory garden?"

"I'm not growing vegetables if that's what you mean."

"What are you growing?"

"Flowers. I don't love the work, mind you. I find it tedious, all the digging and the weeding and the dirt and the watering and the…"

Adam laughed. "So you don't like the digging, the weeding, the dirt, or the watering. Say again why you do it?"

"Because I want to. Because I won't be told what to do with my space. Other people expect me to plant a victory garden, but that doesn't mean I will. I want to use my space on my own terms."

"I understand that," Adam said. "I'm not one to be told what to do, either. Do you like animals?"

"I love animals."

Adam nodded. "Me too. I have a dog right now, George, and last week I found a turtle wandering around Central Park. He looked lonely so I took him home. He lives in my suitcase. I named him Edgar."

"Why Edgar?"

"I don't know. He looks like an Edgar."

I had to laugh since Adam was so earnest about Edgar. "That suitcase must get a lot of use with all the traveling you do with your brothers," I said.

"It does."

We walked in silence for a while, though I kept stealing glances at him, trying to guess what he was thinking. It was hard because his face was no longer an open book as it was during the films. He didn't look cold, Adam. Only thoughtful.

Finally, I asked, "Do you like what you do? Being an actor and traveling all the time?"

"I get paid to play the piano, which I love more than anything. And I get to make people laugh. Did you know it's harder to make people laugh than it is to make them cry?"

"I didn't know that."

"Sure it is. When someone is hurt, people can imagine themselves or their loved ones hurt so they're sad. When someone is dying, everyone cries. But your sense of humor depends on where you grew up, how you're feeling that day, what you do with your life, what you want to do with your life. To get everyone in an audience to laugh at the same thing at the same time is hard, but it's worth the work. The only bad thing, as you've pointed out, is the traveling. I've been in vaudeville since I was 15 years old, and I've crossed the country too many times to count. One of these days I'm gonna bow out of the act and play piano at a movie house again like that kid."

We arrived in front of my red-brown house with the window boxes overflowing with a rainbow scent of flowers. Adam nodded when he saw it. He walked me up the steps to the door.

"It's been a pleasure," he said.

"Thank you for walking me home."

"You know, we're playing the 23rd Street Theater next week. Why don't you come by? I know Max will be glad to see you again, but if he asks you for a date you better turn him down. He's got Roman eyes and Russian hands, if you know what I mean."

Adam jumped the stairs down the stoop and walked some distance before turning back.

"And this time stay awake!"

CHAPTER 6

*T*he next morning I shook my head as I read the paper. The national suffrage movement was at a standstill. Too many suffragists were unsure what the strategy should be during the war. The silent sentinels remained at their posts across from the White House, their words spoken on the banners they held. Mrs. Belmont and those of us on her staff were still on task —we were so close to getting the vote for women in New York— but there was disagreement about whether or not to abandon the national fight for suffrage and assist fully in the war effort. The rationale behind postponing the national effort was this: when the war was over and the men in Congress saw how loyal we were and how we helped during these trying times, they would have to grant us the vote. The rationale for continuing to fight came from those who felt we had been waiting long enough. We were already fighting the same war as the men in combat fatigues so we should continue business as usual. We, too, were making the world safe for democracy. The women did as they would, some stopping the suffrage fight to assist the Red Cross or plant victory gardens. Others, like Cynthia and me, continued our suffrage work.

I remember the morning my father came out of his bedroom

in his terrycloth bathrobe, his terrycloth slippers on his feet. He nodded in my direction without looking at me, his eyes on the green carpeting. He was so distracted he bumped into the sofa, then walked around it as though he hadn't noticed the obstruction. I gestured to the empty chair next to me at the dining room table.

"Sit down, Dad. I'll get you some coffee."

"No need, Rose," said Mrs. Harris as she bustled into the room, coffee pot in hand. "I'll take care of it."

My father sat at the table without taking notice of the coffee cup Mrs. Harris placed in front of him.

"What is it, Dad?"

He shook his head, side to side, again and again, as though the words were inside but he hardly understood them. He tapped an agitated tune on the saucer with a teaspoon while he considered his answer. Finally, he said, "It's martial law, Rose. In the United States of America we have martial law."

"What do you mean?"

"Have you heard of the Espionage Act?"

Mrs. Harris filled my coffee cup and moved my father's cup to the side, just out of his reach. His nervous tin-like melody was becoming monotonous.

"I read about that," Mrs. Harris said. "The fines are pretty steep, aren't they?"

My father nodded. "According to the law, there can be up to $10,000 in fines and 20 years in prison for obstructing military operations in wartime, up to $5,000 in fines and five years in prison for using United States mail in violation of the law."

"Obstructing and violating how?" I asked.

My father paced to the window. His agitation couldn't be contained no matter how far Mrs. Harris moved his coffee cup. He kept the teaspoon in hand to tap a tune on his leg.

"They're not clear about how, and that's what's worrying me. Vague laws mean the government can do whatever it wants however it wants, and it will convince everyone it's right to do so. I have to warn the people, Rose. It's my job to tell them the truth about what's happening."

"You'll be the first to tell people the truth about these laws," I said, "the way you were the first to tell them about Hooverizing."

Hooverizing—named for Herbert Hoover, who was appointed by Woodrow Wilson as the United States Food Administrator—meant sacrificing and going without during this time of war. Hoover believed Americans would willingly cut back on food consumption during the war, alleviating any need to ration. Meatless Mondays were promoted, along with Wheatless Wednesdays and Porkless Thursdays. "Food will win the war," they said. Americans signed pledges at the grocery stores saying they wouldn't waste food. Waste became a dirty word, and to waste was as bad as living without the Patriotism. "Saving Wheat by Saving Meat" and "The Uses of Corn" were popular articles of the day. Americans were urged to eat more chicken and fish instead of beef, which had risen to 50 cents a pound. Meatloaf was to have more loaf than meat, and there was a recipe for victory bread with enough wheat grain to make sandpaper.

My father took the newspaper I had been reading and skimmed the headlines until he found what he was looking for. He folded back the paper and handed it to me. "Have you seen this yet?"

"What is it?" I asked.

"It's the list released by Washington meant to guide responsible citizens."

I read aloud:

"Number one: Observe personal and household economy.

Number two: Urge citizens in private conversation to be patriotic.

Number three: Help organize a Red Cross chapter if there is none in your community.

Number four: Don't be slow to express patriotic sentiments because everyone is either patriotic or not at a time like this.

Number five: Don't get over-excited, but don't suppress your Patriotism—it helps others.

Number six: Keep your American flag displayed from daylight to sunset, but don't allow it to become bedraggled. The flag is what you help to make it."

"The Patriotism is in full force now," my father said. "Infecting everyone like that influenza I keep hearing about. And I don't know what to do about it."

"Keep writing your columns," I said. "People will start paying attention."

"It might be too late, Rose."

I kissed my father's cheek. "Everything will be all right, Dad."

"I hope so."

I checked the time and left the house, late for my walk to school. Suddenly, not far from the brownstone, I noticed how New York City had been flooded by an overflow of soldiers.

The Trans-Atlantic docks along the Hudson River, in Brooklyn and Hoboken, New Jersey, were among those large enough to dock the converted ocean liners that would soon carry thousands of American troops to the western front in France. When the volunteers and draftees were called up, Manhattan became an embarkation camp. The doughboys looked tall in their bulky uniforms with their wide-brimmed, pyramid-topped hats, choking collars, and heavy leggings as they went sightseeing around the city, visiting the theaters along the Great White Way, attending the motion picture palaces, or dancing at the dance rooms. Many Broadway theaters declared themselves Liberty Theaters and offered half-price tickets to the boys in khaki. Many of the young men had never been beyond the boundaries of their small hometowns, and they looked bright-eyed and bushy-tailed as they took trips to Liberty Island or walked the length of Fifth Avenue to bask in the serenity of

Central Park where a captured German submarine was on display.

At school I realized the single teachers had discovered the influx of handsome young doughboys long before I did. In the staff lounge, I listened to the women chat amongst themselves, thinking this must be their chance to find the elusive husbands that had so far eluded them. Two young teachers sat close to each other, their eyes bright, their lips flirty as they giggled over this lieutenant, that captain, or those pretty blue-eyed boys, even if they were only privates.

"After all," Miss Preston reasoned, "how often is the town flooded with available young men?"

How often, indeed, I thought.

Just before the morning bell rang, Miss Avery rushed in, checking her bouffant in the mirror over the sink and pressing an escaped curl into place.

"What is it, Jessica?" Miss Preston asked.

"I'm so flighty today, Ellie," Miss Avery said. "I met up with Christopher this morning, and he asked me to the moving pictures, but I think I already made plans with William, or was it Donald? I honestly can't remember. Golly, what a silly goof I am! And I think I gave my number to another boy too."

Miss Preston nodded to Miss Steward, with her left hand conspicuously displayed on her teacup. "Have you heard Miss Steward is going to be married next week?"

"Next week!" said Miss Avery. "That's very soon, Margaret."

"Robert proposed last night," Miss Steward said. She smiled with great condescension, looking every bit the matron she was soon going to be.

"I thought you were seeing someone called Daniel," I said.

Miss Steward turned her condescension onto me. "That was last month, dear. I've been seeing Robert for three weeks now."

"A whole three weeks," I said. "Where is he from?"

"He's from a factory-owning family in Michigan, or a restaurant-owning family in Missouri. Or is it a farm-owning family in Kansas or Alabama? We don't talk about things like that."

"What do you talk about?" I asked.

"Oh, you know, everything."

The morning bell rang, and Mrs. Rittenhouse walked in. I had seen her standing in the open doorway listening to the chatter and I was certain Mrs. Rittenhouse, the conservator of appearances, would warn the ladies that their behavior wasn't acceptable during school hours or on school property. Instead, she said, "Miss Scofield, I must speak to you."

"The bell rang," I said. "The children are waiting for me."

"Mrs. Hallerston is minding the children. I need a moment of your time."

I followed her into her office, and she sat like a queen taking her throne. Even at her height, and she was tall, Mrs. Rittenhouse, I thought she needed a step stool to see over her mahogany desk.

"Miss Scofield, I'm afraid your involvement with the suffrage movement is becoming widely known, and it's not good for the children." She lowered her spectacles to the tip of her nose and looked at me as though she were the teacher and I were a wayward student. "Children shouldn't have such nonsense as teachers worried about votes for women."

"My involvement with the suffrage movement is my concern," I said.

"If your attention is on the suffrage movement, then they cannot be here. You cannot be here and there at the same time, Miss Scofield. All your energies should be focused on this school and these children."

"I don't neglect my duties here," I said. "When I'm here all my energies are directed on these children. But I do have a life outside this building. There are hours in my day that aren't filled with this job, hours that are mine to do with as I please."

"That's true enough, seeing as you don't have a family of your own."

I sighed. "How I spend those hours is my business. Even you can't tell me how to use my free time."

Mrs. Rittenhouse smiled the same smile she showed to the parents who tried to convince her to put their two-year-old into kindergarten. Because they offered enough money the little boy was now in Hilde's class. It was a dangerous smile.

"If the parents disapprove of your involvement then they'll pull their children out of the school," Mrs. Rittenhouse said. "If one parent pulls her child out, then others with similar opinions will follow."

"But it's my responsibility as a teacher to show the children that this is a country where we have rights. We can make changes that add to the quality of our lives."

"We cannot have a teacher who detracts from our job at hand, and that job is educating our children."

Mrs. Rittenhouse turned her attention to the pile of papers always on her desk. She picked up a pen and began writing, engrossed in her work as though I were no longer there. But I wouldn't be dismissed that way.

"Are you saying my job is in jeopardy if I continue with the suffrage movement?" I asked.

"I'm saying the children are our first priority."

"The children are always my first priority."

"The children must understand how we're fighting to help those overseas who cannot help themselves, the mothers, the children, the old lame men who are being murdered in their homes while they sleep. They must see how we're fighting to make sure those horrid people don't come here and do the same to us."

"So we're to scare the children as their parents are being scared?"

"We are 100% American."

Mrs. Rittenhouse looked at the Stars and Stripes hanging above her head and seemed to draw strength from it. It looked more like a vaudeville act than a genuine response, I thought. Mr.

Rittenhouse walked in, a sweater-wearing, slouch-shouldered, mustached man on the other side of middle-aged. He nodded at me, bowed toward his wife, and disappeared down the hall. I always thought he was a kind, sympathetic man, with his downcast eyes and gentle smile, a former teacher himself, and I thought it was unfortunate he lived in the shadows of this silly woman because of a poor choice when he was young and foolish and looking for a comfortable life.

I watched Mrs. Rittenhouse, who acted as though the papers on her desk blocked her view of me, and I was flooded with disdain for her. I had always managed to explain away the problems I saw daily around the school because I liked my job and I loved the children. When parents came in complaining the school was too hot and their little Johnnies would burn up, Mrs. Rittenhouse removed her sweater and wiped her forehead, saying, "Absolutely, it's too hot and I'll see to it myself it's cooled down." When the next parents complained it was too cold and their Sallies would freeze to death, she put her sweater on and shivered and said, "Absolutely, it's too cold and I'll see to it myself it's warmed up." Everything was about appeasing the parents—and spending as little money as possible on the school. There were days when I needed to count the crackers each child received at snack time because there wasn't enough for them to have more than one. There were days when I had to split the crackers into halves or thirds and explain to the still-hungry children how the kitchen cupboards were bare. I felt like the orphanage master in *Oliver Twist* when I had to deny their pleas for more. I shook my head and walked to my classroom. When I left after the afternoon bell rang, I saw Mr. and Mrs. Rittenhouse drive away in a new two-toned Cadillac. At least the money from the school was going to a good cause, I thought.

I spent the rest of the afternoon shopping for a new spring-wear dress at Altman's. I bought a charmeuse dress with red and white stripes and a bright red satin jacket with a straw cloth hat with red satin trim and an organza bow. The redness of the outfit was louder than the earth tones other women found fashionable then, and even when I tried it on I knew I might never wear it, but the happiness of the red appealed to me and I bought it anyway.

From Altman's I walked to the Waldorf-Astoria, the red brick and sandstone hotel built in the German Renaissance style. Whenever I dined there I entertained myself by watching the cultural elite, many of whom, like the Carters, lived along Millionaire's Row on Fifth Avenue. They chewed and swallowed their food as I did, even if they held their heads at an awkwardly high angle and their shoulders rigid, as Mrs. Carter had instructed me during our afternoon tea. The women in their fine silks and jewels talked through their noses while the men in ducks and derbies talked through their wallets. As I lingered over a watercress salad I wondered if these women were following the paths their hearts set for them. Certainly, they were living the lives little girls were taught to dream of—the fairy tale that came from marrying a well-to-do prince. Certainly, they were materially provided for—their fingers, wrists, and necks dripped with rainbow-colored stones, their handbags, parasols, shoes, hats, and dresses were all from the finest materials. They had expensive automobiles for their chauffeurs to drive, nannies for their children's care, and maids for their wealthy-style homes. These were women with nothing to do, of which their husbands boasted proudly, because the less their wives had to do the more successful the husbands had been.

Seeing nothing more at lunch to entertain me, I took my shopping bags home, and, finding the brownstone empty, I left to wander around Central Park, which felt Eden-like in contrast to the crowded, impersonal cityscape. The green grounds appealed to me as I meandered the tree-shaded walks, and then I sat on a secluded bench in the gazebo of the Ladies' Pavilion, watching the automobiles and the pedestrians in the streets, the birds and the ducks in the ponds, the groves and the flowers growing wild in the grass. Drifting and dreaming in the dimpled light, I began to think about the waiting.

The waiting began long ago, long ago before women knew they were waiting. There was a time before time when women, with their blood, their tears, and their powers to bring forth new life, were thought awesome. They weren't waiting, submissive, ordered about and unconsidered by. They were revered, idolized, worshipped, feared.

They were mother-goddesses, respected before the waiting.

Then the waiting began. Staying behind, outside of the obvious economy, fetching water to drink, baking bread to eat, creating a home of comfort to live in, and bringing new generations into being—these were important and necessary but marginalized, looked down upon. These women were too tired to know they were waiting. Watered, wrinkled hands and tired, dark-lined eyes quickly lost the bloom of life-giving blood—these were the visual signs of their waiting. The unfulfilled heart made heavy with misuse and disrespect, the unfulfilled desires no one would see but she could feel, this was the internal self-struggle with waiting. Then, they were waiting and silent because they had no way to communicate their waiting, their voices left mute.

The men who made economy also made technology, mostly for war, mostly to bring blood and kill better than those not as technologically advanced as they. To kill better, that was the intention behind technology, but the practical result of these new-fangled machines was that life became easier. The waiting women knew this. Baking bread and cooking meals no longer took all the daylight hours. Iceboxes made the time-consuming task of preserving food for winter no longer necessary. Telephones made appearances to call on neighbors no longer necessary. Women could send their voices wherever they wanted, whenever they wanted, and this was wonderful for them. Trains and planes made travel easy, available. The arrival of the Model T made land-distance travel affordable. Male, female, tall, short, slim, stout—

anyone could go anywhere within the ocean boundaries. Both working women and leisurely women found they had more of the most valuable commodity available: time. Confinement became nostalgia. Women made appearances in the world.

Suddenly, women knew they were waiting, and as soon as they knew they were waiting they no longer wanted to. The voices they had begun to share in song, in literature, in friendship and sisterhood and loving mother words, these voices, our voices, were now directed, with vehemence, toward Washington. We weren't demanding special attention or extra privileges. We weren't demanding a return to mother-goddess days. We wanted our due after being left aside for so long. We wanted representation, but more than that, we wanted, no, demanded recognition.

I lost myself gazing at a small child, a girl in plaits, running along the grass-grown dandelions near the pond. The child was beaming and I thought she was beautiful. I felt a pang, I wasn't sure where, somewhere deep within, and I stared at the child and wondered what it would be like to be her mother.

It was difficult for me to visualize mothers or mothering. I knew what it was like to be kept warm in a father's arms, but I could never be a father. I could be a mother, but how good would I be at something I hadn't seen since I was two? Still, at a certain age one loses the claim of neglect or the dislike of the fates. At a certain age one can no longer complain "My parents did" or "My parents didn't." When you become an adult you learn to put the past in its place, its appropriate place with the understanding that it was your past that led you to who you are today, but then you move forward, pushing if you have to, looking toward tomorrow and the tomorrow after that. When do people become adults? When they're able to look to the future without regretting the past. That is what I wanted to do. I didn't have a mother, and I was determined not to regret it.

When I was young I didn't have dreams of future offspring with names like Johnny or Katie. I didn't play house with displays of imaginary tea. I didn't carry baby dolls that needed pretend milk or invisible applesauce. Was it because I had no mother with babies in fleece blankets? I had no one to hold close and nuzzle, no one to respond to soft, pure kisses. I hadn't seen the mother instinct at work for herself. I saw friends whose mothers had babies to cuddle, but I thought the desire to have babies to coo over was part of woman's weakness, her curse, one of the many jokes nature, Mother Nature, had played on us. Our Mother has created us to be left aside as inferior, I thought. The girl with the plaits went by, giggling, glowing, and reaching for the spring-green leaves as they swayed in the high-away branches. I felt that pang again and knew this pang, its understanding and its fulfillment, was one more thing resigned to the waiting.

As the sun began to set and the sky glowed pink on the horizon, I left my bench by the dandelions and the ducks and made my way to the theater where I witnessed my friends, the five hurricanes, in action. They were everything my father raved about—entertaining and musical—and they enjoyed themselves as much as their audience enjoyed them. After their performance I made my way backstage with my father's credentials, and the circus-like, smoke-filled atmosphere engulfed me.

"You're the dame who slept through our act!"

It was Jacob, escorting the waitress from the diner. I smiled at him while I scanned the faces and listened to the voices. I felt a hand on my arm and turned to see wide gray eyes looking into mine.

"Hells bells! I trust you found our meager display satisfactory enough this evening to keep your eyes open?"

"Now I know why my father can't stop raving about you," I said to Max. "You boys are so talented."

"Where is he, anyhow? Your old man, I mean." Max drew closer and didn't let go of my arm.

"He's late at the office tonight and couldn't come." As I spoke, David took my other arm.

"Hey!" said Max. "I found her first."

"23 Skidoo!" David answered, though he immediately found solace with a pretty girl from the ballet act. So, it seemed, had Adam.

Adam was in the corner, huddled close to two of the blond-haired, long-legged ballerinas in their too-small tutus with their too-wide smiles. One of them, the taller, blonder of the two, returned his attention with fluttering lashes and flirting lips. The girls were throwing their heads back and flipping their curls from their faces so he could see the blushing men found so seductive.

Max was talking to me, but I only nodded as I watched Adam flirt with the dancers. The flirting was a dance in itself, with Adam taking the lead. Max must have sensed my attentions were elsewhere, so he excused himself to the poker game always waging somewhere backstage. I caught eyes with Adam, who looked startled when he saw me. When he realized I was leaving he stepped away from the ballerinas and asked, "You want I should walk you home?"

"That's all right," I said. I looked at the ballerinas, who were watching us and whispering to each other. "You're busy."

As I left he turned back to the girls I found foolish but he found friendly and willing.

CHAPTER 7

𝓘t was summer in the city and the lightness of spring was traded for heavy, unfriendly air. Automobiles overheated. Crowded city dwellers had shorter tempers than usual while gentlemen and gentle ladies dabbed at perspiring foreheads with monogrammed handkerchiefs. The young soldiers who looked like boys playing dress-up in their fathers' fatigues looked flushed as they did their sightseeing along the Manhattan streets. Even the pigeons were weighted down with humidity. Hats drooped, pompadours drooped, clothing, too tight to allow the wearers to breathe comfortably, drooped. Many sought relief in boxy bathing suits along the seashore, at amusement parks like Coney Island, under the blooming trees at Central Park, or by leaving the city altogether. Many ignored the tangible air and worked in their gardens, some helping the vegetables they had sown so, come fall, their victory gardens would provide bountiful harvests, allowing our men in khaki to find success on the western front.

With Cynthia's help, I continued to sow my own seeds. I planted two more rosebushes, one pink and one white, and around the roses I planted wildflowers that would bloom blue, yellow, and red as I used my space my way, regardless of the mean-spirited looks from neighbors who, while planting their victory gardens, stretched their necks over the wall to see what I was doing. I ignored their titters and spoke to Cynthia when she was planting beside me. Sometimes we listened to the Victrola, and the treble tunes of "Oh, You Beautiful Doll" or "I Want a Girl Just Like the Girl That Married Dear Old Dad" sprinkled the oppressive summer with some melody of relief. I ignored the loud whispers from others about how there were no vegetables in my garden, only wasteful flowers. They didn't understand the true meaning of a victory garden, though to be fair neither did I.

As 1917 continued it became a crime, a felony, not to be infected with the Patriotism. Newspapers with pacifist tendencies were closing due to lack of funds or the government shut them down. My father said not to worry about him since no one in the government would pay him any mind.

"I'm not important enough to fuss over," he said. "I write a local column for a local newspaper."

"Your local newspaper happens to be the *New York Times,*" I said.

"My readership has dwindled, Rosie. I don't know how much longer I'll be there."

"Have they said anything to you?"

My father shook his head. "I have a feeling it's coming."

"But you won't stop writing your columns," I said.

"Someone has to be the voice of reason."

Suddenly, there was less to occupy my days. School was out for the summer. With Cynthia's help my rosebushes bloomed and scented the backyard. There was little left for the suffragists to do in New York but wait for the election, which Mrs. Belmont assured us would grant New York women the right to vote. I heard about the new game police played in Washington, arresting the women standing peaceably outside the White House gates with their banners that read: Mr. President, What Will You Do For Women Suffrage? The women were jailed, and when they were refused the political prisoner status they believed they deserved they took their cue from their British counterparts and refused to eat. If they couldn't get their due one way, they would try another. I shuddered as I read about prison cells and force-feedings, and my claustrophobia raged within me. I was proud of their courage, but I thought I could never be that brave.

Women weren't the only ones using silence to make their point. On July 28, 1917, 15,000 people walked down Fifth Avenue to protest racial discrimination and violence. I watched the procession from the curb and wished them well. I saw the similarities in the fight for equality for Blacks and women, but I understood the differences as well. The discrimination and violence that Blacks suffered were in so many ways more difficult. For a while, the two movements worked together toward the common goal of liberty and justice for all, but there were misunderstandings and accusations, and eventually the movements separated though we had been stronger together.

After the procession, I headed to Times Square and my usual seat on the balcony of the Rialto Theater. When I arrived upstairs I found Adam laughing at the Little Tramp twitching his black mustache, waddling about, twirling his cane, getting himself into and out of trouble. I thought Adam looked lonely so I moved to the seat behind him and said, "Hey! I'm the dame who slept through your whole act!"

"Hi, Rose."

"Where is the ballerina?" I whispered.

"What ballerina?"

"That pretty blonde who wouldn't leave you alone long enough to say goodbye to me. That ballerina." Adam's face was blank, unremembering. "You know, the one with the big..."

"Smile?"

"Yes, the one with the big smile."

"One dame's smile is pretty much like the next."

"She's one of many for you, I see."

Adam shrugged, though it wasn't the gesture of pride I had seen from his brothers, and I was tempted to tease him some more. I looked for verdigris green but all I saw were waves of unruly chestnut.

We fell silent as the newsreels displayed war and death like there was nothing else anywhere in the world to know. Adam pointed to the seat next to him, so I sat there. In the enclosed darkness of a half-empty balcony with only flickering shades of gray for light and tinkering piano music for sound, it felt as though we were alone. As the newsreels finished rolling Adam leaned close and said, "I offered to walk you home but you turned me down." He had a quiet voice, Adam, and he never pressed to be heard.

"Yes," I said, "I did."

"You shouldn't turn down a nice guy when he offers to walk you home. You might end up walking with someone like Max or Stuart. Max thinks you're some cute bird."

"I'd rather walk alone."

"I'm privileged, then, because already I've walked you home."

"You're certainly more polite to me than you were to that ballerina you were pawing. What's wrong? Isn't my smile big enough for you?"

"Your smile is fine, honey, just beautiful. But it's different than other girls who flaunt their teeth all over the place. Sure, they get a guy's attention for a day, a week, a month even, but not much else. Now here you are in your high-buttoned blouse and your gray watching eyes and you seem far away, like you're saving your smile for some other time. What are you waiting for?"

"I don't know. I only know I'm waiting."

"We're all waiting one way or another," Adam said. "But how will you know when you've found what you're waiting for?"

I couldn't answer him because I didn't know.

Adam walked me home that afternoon. When we arrived at the red-brown brownstone I invited him in for tea, my way of prolonging the afternoon. Inside, Adam clapped when he saw the wind-up Victrola next to the window, and when I went into the kitchen to help Mrs. Harris fix the tea I heard piano music, the beauty of melody and harmony. I hummed along as I poured boiling water over spoonfuls of pekoe and tried to place which recording Adam had put on the turntable. When I brought the tea into the sitting room I realized the music wasn't from the Victrola but from Adam. He had found his way to the upright piano, the one my father had been neglecting since the war began. The song Adam played in the lower octaves was soft, slow, and gentle, much like him. Not mournful, not ever mournful, but with feeling.

The Adam Bell sitting before the piano, his eyes closed, his fingers caressing the black and white keys as though in religious invocation, wasn't the Adam I thought I knew. He was far away, absorbed by the song emanating from somewhere deep within him, where he really was. His breath came in time with the music, and the music pulled its essence, its life, from him. I thought I should leave because Adam making music that way seemed too personal to witness without feeling as if I were spying on someone who thought he was alone. There was Adam, the piano, the music, and nothing else. When he opened his eyes to stare through the brownstone wall to the beauty on the other side, I saw poetry in his eyes, and I thought the walls leaned closer, straining to hear every note. For those moments my home became a cathedral where glory was sung to the wonders of the world.

When Mrs. Harris brought out cakes and tarts, Adam stopped playing. He helped himself to a slice of lemon pound cake, and he savored every bite of it.

"I haven't eaten like this since my mother died," he said. He smiled at Mrs. Harris, and she giggled the way she did when the butcher flirted with her.

"You look familiar, Mr. Bell," Mrs. Harris said as she refilled his teacup. "Have I seen you somewhere before?"

"Do you go to the theaters on Broadway?" he asked.

"Of course."

"You wouldn't have seen me there. We don't play Broadway yet. We're in vaudeville. You probably saw our posters around town."

Adam noticed the photograph of Cynthia on the mantelpiece and nodded toward it. "You look like your mother."

"That's my aunt. My mother died years ago."

"Where's a picture of your mother?"

I looked at the mantelpiece. "I don't know." I remembered one behind more recent photos, so I pulled it out and showed him.

"She's lovely," he said. "Why keep it back where no one can see?"

"That's where it's always been."

Adam took the photograph and inspected every detail. I was interested in what he saw so I looked too. I saw a dark-haired woman with dark, round eyes looking directly into the camera. I was startled by the sight of her.

"She doesn't look weak," I said.

"Why should she?"

"She died of the consumption. She died because she was weak."

Adam studied my mother's photograph some more. "What was she like?"

"I don't remember much about her. I was two when she died. My father used to try to talk to me about her, even my aunt tried sometimes, but I wasn't interested. I wanted to be a woman on my own terms."

"Why can't you be a woman on your own terms and remember your mother at the same time?" I shrugged, the only answer I had.

But Adam wouldn't give up. "I bet you could remember some-thing about her if you tried."

I looked at the photograph, hoping that seeing it for the first time in years would trigger some misplaced memory, but I had nothing, my mind a void. Adam stayed silent, waiting, and I could tell by his easy expression that he would stand there an hour if that was how long it took me to give him an answer. I closed my eyes and held that picture of my mother in my mind. Suddenly, I saw her, a faint vision tugging at the edge of my memory, as if I saw her through a blurred camera lens. I said what I saw, without editing, without worrying. Even though I didn't know Adam well, I trusted him. Instinctively, I knew he would understand what I was trying to tell him, disjointed though my memories were.

"I see a pale-skinned woman with upswept dark hair and a white-pearl smile with her arms stretched toward me. I see her leaning over flowers, savoring their fruity fragrance. I hear the sound of her lilted laughter."

"What do you feel when you think of her?"

"I don't have any feelings connected to her."

"Nothing?"

"Nothing."

"Not any joy, any love, not even any sadness at her loss?"

I shut my eyes tighter and concentrated on the darkness behind my eyelids. What did I feel about that dark-haired woman with the white-pearl smile with her arms stretched toward me? I opened my eyes and shook my head.

"Nothing," I said. "It feels odd, looking at that photograph, knowing that woman is my mother and not feeling anything. It's why she's never been real to me. It's like I have memories of some random dark-haired woman."

"You need to think about her more, Rose. Then she'll become more real to you."

Adam took the photograph back, studied it more, and nodded. "I was right the first time. You look like your mother."

Mrs. Harris brought a fresh pot of tea into the room. She looked at the photograph in Adam's hands. "Are you talking about Mrs. Scofield? That woman was sweet as sugar and feisty as yeast. She knew who she was in the world and Mr. Scofield loved her dearly for it."

"You never told me that before," I said.

"You never wanted to hear it."

Adam handed me the photograph. He led me to the mantelpiece where he rearranged the other pictures and found a place for my mother front and center.

"You should look at her once in a while," he said.

"I will."

Someone knocked at the door, and Mrs. Harris hurried away to answer it. She came back a moment later trying to suppress a grin and not succeeding.

"Mr. Montgomery Carter is here," she said. She winked at me as she disappeared into the kitchen.

"Who's that?" Adam whispered.

"Of the Fifth Avenue Carters," I said.

Montgomery appeared, a bouquet of blushing roses in his hand. He removed his derby and bowed in my direction. He looked surprised when he saw Adam, and he managed a curt nod. He handed me the bouquet.

"I hope you don't feel I'm being too forward, Miss Scofield, but I saw these and thought of you. I was compelled to bring them to you before they lost a moment of their beauty. They are your namesakes after all."

I breathed in the silky scent. "They're lovely, Mr. Carter. Thank you. Let me put these into some water."

Mrs. Harris bustled into the room. "No need. I'll take care of that. Such a beautiful bouquet." She leaned close and whispered, "And I bet they cost a pretty penny too." She bustled out as quickly as she bustled in, leaving me alone with two men who couldn't have been more opposite. Montgomery was eyeing Adam like an officer on the battlefield sizing up his opponent. How much damage could Adam do to him before he could damage in return? Adam seemed amused by Montgomery and not particularly bothered by the man's sudden appearance. Adam leaned against the wall, his hands in his pockets, waiting for Montgomery to make the first move.

"Mr. Carter," I said, "this is my friend Adam Bell. Adam, this is Montgomery Carter."

"Of the Fifth Avenue Carters," Adam said.

"You're familiar with my family then."

Adam shook his head. "Never heard of you."

I gestured toward the sofa. "Would you like to sit down?"

"I can only stay a minute," Montgomery Carter said. "Your father is keeping me very busy in the office, I'm afraid. I've told him it isn't necessary to work every hour of the day, but he seems bent on fixing things that don't need fixing."

"Such as?" I asked.

"Such as speaking out against the war. Every rational person came to realize the necessity of this war a long time ago. He's not winning himself any readers with his lack of Patriotism. He's losing readers every day, and they're very vocal when they write complaining letters to the editor."

"My father is stubborn when he's right," I said.

Adam smiled at me. "And so are you."

"Yes. And so am I."

Montgomery Carter cleared his throat. "But your father means well, and as my mother says, allowances must be made for those who mean well."

"Rose here is just like her father," Adam said.

"How do you mean?" asked Mr. Carter.

"She works with the suffrage movement. She's rather brave to do something others don't agree with."

"Do you think the suffrage movement is an appropriate way for a young woman to bide her time?" Montgomery Carter asked.

"What business is it of mine?" Adam answered. "As long as she's not in any bodily danger, she can do what she likes."

Montgomery Carter looked remarkably like his mother when he nodded in that patronizing way. I expected him to start clucking his tongue. "I see," he said, though it was obvious from his flat tone he didn't see at all. He sat on the edge of the sofa, his arms crossed over his chest, his expression amused. "Tell me again what you do, Mr. Bell?"

"What I do?"

"Yes, for employment. I assume you're employed, though you're here in the middle of the day as though you have nothing whatever else to do."

"I'm an entertainer."

"And what kind of entertaining do you do?"

"Have you ever been to the burlesque theaters?"

"I most certainly have not."

"Me either. No vaudevillian would ever dare appear on a burlesque stage. It's a disgrace even the Five Bell Brothers wouldn't stoop to, and we've stooped pretty low, let me tell you. We wouldn't play top banana in a burlesque if you paid us. I slip and slide enough as it is."

"I'm sure you've received some pies in the face in your day," Montgomery Carter said.

"Not me. Now my little brother Jakey…"

Mr. Carter turned to me. "Were you aware that Mr. Bell is a vaudevillian?"

"I'm very much aware of it. My father and I saw them perform and they're one of the funniest acts out there."

Adam leaned toward me. "You fell asleep, remember?"

"I saw you the second time."

Adam nodded. "That's right."

Montgomery Carter watched Adam and me as though he didn't know what to make of us, as though we were visitors from another planet who spoke a language he couldn't learn. I glanced at the clock on the mantelpiece and smiled at Montgomery Carter.

"Didn't you say my father was expecting you?" I asked.

Mr. Carter pulled the round gold watch from the gold chain attached to his waistcoat pocket and checked the time. He stood from the sofa.

"If you'll excuse me, Miss Scofield. You're correct. Your father is expecting me back at the office." He looked at Adam. "I'm sure you understand how times like ours are quite busy for those of us in the newspaper business. I have several pressing items that need tending to."

"I have no doubt about it," said Adam.

Montgomery Carter returned his derby to his head, and I followed him to the door. When we stepped outside he turned to me.

"My mother has requested your presence at a dinner party at our home this Friday evening at 6 p.m. precisely. I'm looking forward to seeing you there." He gave a last glance at Adam, who was waiting patiently inside, and shook his head. Then he grabbed my hand, kissed it, and backed away.

"Mr. Carter," I said, "I don't think…"

"I'll see you Friday evening, Miss Scofield. Good afternoon."

Before I could protest any more he disappeared into the long black car waiting by the curb. Adam joined me by the door, watching while Montgomery was driven away.

"He's a pleasant sort of fellow," Adam said.

"Is he?"

"He likes you."

I shook my head, trying to shake Adam's words away like dust from my hair. "He doesn't."

"He does. You're a lucky girl. Looks like he's loaded."

I sighed. "Lucky me."

That night as I lay in bed under a moonless window I thought about Adam Bell and his large, expression-filled eyes, his joy-filled smile, and I compared him to the lackluster reality of Montgomery Carter. When Adam played the piano he radiated melody and poetry. When Montgomery Carter walked into the room he deflated any good spirits as if he had popped air from a balloon. Adam wasn't handsome in the usual sense of well-defined features. He wasn't the kind of man who would catch your attention when he entered the room the way Montgomery Carter did. Adam didn't have a movie star's aura, broad shoulders or obvious cheekbones like Montgomery Carter, features that normally attract attention. Adam wasn't obtrusive or intrusive. He didn't look taller when he was standing on his money the way Montgomery Carter did, mainly because he didn't have much. Adam wasn't immediately obvious, but he was eventually obvious. Whenever I sensed his presence I was drawn to him, his bright eyes, his friendliness.

I climbed out of bed and looked at myself in the floor-length mirror. What I saw looking back usually depended on my mood. That night I saw, if not a beautiful young woman, then at least a well-groomed young woman with a pleasing smile and an honest manner. In the worry-filled quiet, though, I also saw a young woman who was growing older. When I leaned closer to my reflection I saw the beginning lines that would become deeper, then wrinkle. My inquisitive nature meant I was always thinking, so two vertical lines formed between my brows. Not long before I noticed silver, wiry strands that clashed with the red-brown shade I had always known to be mine. For now, I could cut away the offensive strands and pretend I had never seen them, though that couldn't continue forever.

What did Montgomery Carter of the Fifth Avenue Carters see in me that attracted him? Surely, he could find someone prettier, richer, better suited to society. Adam didn't have problems finding blonder, prettier girls, even if they were ballerinas. Certainly, Montgomery Carter could find someone more suited to his lifestyle. What about that toilet paper heiress my father heard about? She would have been perfect for him, I was sure of it.

I went back to bed, though I didn't sleep much that night, wondering what had happened that afternoon and what any of it meant. As I drifted to sleep, I decided it didn't matter. None of it mattered as long as I was still waiting.

CHAPTER 8

*1*918 began with a continuing bend toward optimism as Wilson was inaugurated for a second term. Now, with the khaki-colored presence of young soldiers, people believed our boys would end the war of all wars, the Great War. They believed the presence of the Stars and Stripes along the barbed-wire trenches of the western front in France would stop the machine-gunning, the air-dropping, and the killing over there.

The 1917-1918 winter was the coldest in memory. The wartime lack of wood and coal meant many shivered in the night, and those who didn't shiver hardly noticed those who did. Still, most people moved into the new year with optimism, intent on waving their home-sized flags to the glory of democracy. Tell your friends and neighbors to speak well of our country, the government exclaimed. Be 100% American.

100% Americans were expected to tattle on those who didn't display their flags from their homes or who spoke against the war. 100% American women volunteered at Red Cross stations along the front lines or at home. Only the uncouth would say aloud what everyone knew—that some of these 100% American nurses had gone overseas to find 100% American husbands. Of course, not all women volunteers had such selfish motives, and many went to tend blinded, gas-filled eyes or bloodied, gangrened wounds or amputations or deaths. In the trenches, on a stretcher, in a hospital cot, it didn't matter where the dying lay, it was dying all the same. There were women with the Red Cross because it was in their hearts to help, to wipe away sweat, tears, and blood, to feed, bathe, comfort, and care. Perhaps a few young women went overseas thinking that if the ceremony were performed before the ether wore off then their soldier-husbands wouldn't know the difference.

At school, the Stars and Stripes fell from every corner of the building. The textbook room was nearly bare, having been emptied of any book with any semblance of having been written by or about anyone of German ancestry, as well as any book that might not awaken the glorifying ideals of democracy in young, impressionable minds. I remember the day I walked into my classroom after the winter holiday and found my three long shelves of children's books dwindled to one short line.

Then Hilde was fired. Monday she was there, and Tuesday she was gone, a substitute teacher in her place. After school I went to Mrs. Rittenhouse and demanded to know what had become of Hilde.

"You know how I feel about her," Mrs. Rittenhouse said. "She's a lovely girl, but Mr. Rittenhouse felt she wasn't good for the children. It's not good for the children to have such nonsense as teachers who are enemies of our nation."

"Hilde is a loyal American citizen," I said.

"She is German. That is all Mr. Rittenhouse needs to know to make the proper decision."

Mrs. Rittenhouse pushed her silver-tipped spectacles to the bridge of her nose, then picked up her pen and busied herself with her ever-present paperwork. But I wouldn't be dismissed.

"I don't understand why Hilde, the most patient and caring of all the teachers here, should lose her job because of which country she happened to be born in. She loves this country. She loves what it stands for. She has her papers if you need to see them."

"Papers can be fabricated, Miss Scofield."

"There are no people more loyal to this country than the Eberhardts," I said.

Mrs. Rittenhouse looked at me over her spectacles, her eyes squints, her lips pulled into her mouth, but I learned integrity from my father and would rather speak out and risk the consequences than stay silent and, by my reticence, surrender to something I didn't believe in.

Mrs. Rittenhouse shook her head. I thought she was ready to call me nearly impudent as Mrs. Carter had. "Mr. Rittenhouse has decided to require every teacher in our employment to sign a loyalty oath to this country."

"Hilde would have signed such an oath immediately."

Mrs. Rittenhouse sighed as though the problems of the world weighed her down. "I'm afraid it's true. Traitors and conspirators against this country wouldn't scruple to lie in that way."

"If you're having teachers sign an oath to show their loyalty, then why…"

Mrs. Rittenhouse held up her hand. "I wouldn't expect you to understand the perplexities we're faced with. All I can say for certain is you must curtail your involvement with the suffrage movement or we may need to release you as well. It's not very American to be fighting for the vote now, is it?"

"I'm not currently involved in the movement," I said. "The women's suffrage law has already passed here in New York."

"By a margin of 100 votes, thanks to the Tammany Hall precinct leaders."

"Thanks to whoever helped get the vote for women. You can vote now, Mrs. Rittenhouse. Isn't that the most American ideal of all, the ability to have your voice heard?"

Mrs. Rittenhouse grasped my hand as though she hadn't heard my last words. "You're no longer with the suffrage movement?

That's wonderful news, Miss Scofield. I'm so glad you're finally thinking like a loyal American. Mr. Rittenhouse and I didn't want to lose you."

"I'm sure you didn't," I said. I couldn't even fake a smile as I pulled my hand away.

SATURDAY MORNING I was awoken by chirping outside my window that sounded like absent-minded songbirds. When I looked outside I knew I was right. Standing on the stoop, gesturing widely with their arms, singing in well-intentioned harmony, were the Five Bell Brothers:

Hail! Hail! The gang's all here,
What the deuce do we care,
What the deuce do we care,
Hail! Hail! We're full of cheer,
What the deuce do we care, Bill!

My father opened the front door. "Boys! Welcome!"

When I went downstairs I found my father, his gap-toothed grin wide, engrossed in stories the brothers shared about their recent escapades down South. Max spoke about two sisters he and Jacob picked up in front of a theater in Alabama.

"Freesheeting it's called," Max said.

"Why freesheeting?" I asked.

"Because whenever the performers are on the prowl for the opposite sex we stick ourselves to the walls outside the theater to advertise ourselves."

"You know," said David, "the way our posters advertise our acts."

"We stand there," Max explained, "so the cute chicks walking by know we're actors. We leave our make-up on after the show for the same reason."

"I thought people don't care for actors," I said.

Max grinned. "People don't, but dames do."

David nodded. "Especially in Birmingham."

"What happened in Birmingham?" my father asked.

"We met these pretty little sisters who were more than willing to keep company with me and Jacob one night and Stuart the next…"

Adam shook his head. "You and your mouth, Maxie. There's a lady here."

"I don't mind," I said, "though I'm not sure what Stuart's wife would say about the situation. Aren't you married, Stuart?"

"He doesn't seem to remember that when we're on the road," Jacob said.

Stuart shrugged but didn't look otherwise concerned. I looked at Adam, who nodded toward his brother as if to say, that's Stuart and we love him anyway. Then Adam stood from the sofa and gestured for me to follow him. As we walked into the kitchen he peeked into the pocket of his oversized raincoat and patted it.

"I brought you a present," he said. He reached into his pocket and pulled out a brown and white ball of fur with whiskers and round blue eyes. I took the kitten and held her close, feeling the warm fur purring against my neck.

"I found her in the gutter outside my apartment. I've been taking care of her, but we're going back on the road soon. I want her to have a permanent home, so I thought of you." He added, somewhat shyly, "I hope you don't mind. I named her Molly."

"I like the name Molly," I said.

"I thought you would."

I took down a bowl from the cupboard and filled it with milk. I put the kitten on the floor next to the bowl and she lapped up the milk with her tiny pink tongue.

"I don't know if you heard," Adam said, "but we came to tell your father the good news. We're playing the Palace."

"That's the Big Time," I said.

"Most people know the reputation of the Palace. Everyone's a performer after all."

I laughed. "I'm no performer. I'm a teacher."

"You don't put on a show to get the kids' attention in class? Sure you do. I perform on a stage for the entertainment of others, that's all."

"You have a talent for that," I said.

"Don't forget, I've been at it for 14 years. I didn't have a talent for anything when my brothers and I started. But I kept trying, and I watched other performers, and I tried out different routines, and I practiced, and I got better. Some performers use their talents to push themselves forward in the world while others go into the world anyway and hope their talent catches up. We fall into the second category."

"But all the hard work has paid off, Adam."

"I don't know how much we had to do with it," Adam said. "Seems the reviews your dad kept writing for us finally got to Albee. Albee's giving us the stage next Wednesday."

The dream of every vaudeville performer was to appear at E.F. Albee's Palace Theater on Broadway. Only those with their talent intact made it to that illustrious stage. The theater's alumnus included such notables as Douglas Fairbanks, Will Rogers, Ethel Barrymore, W.C. Fields, Eva Tanguay—the "I don't care girl" with her manic manner and mop of blond hair—Sophie Tucker—the last of the "red hot mamas"—and the Four Marx Brothers. Now the Five Bell Brothers would be counted among vaudeville royalty.

My father came into the kitchen and shuffled through a few drawers. "Have you seen the cards and the poker chips, Rose?" I went to the cupboard above the icebox and took down two red decks of playing cards and the poker chips. "The boys and I are going to pass the morning playing a few hands. You, too, Adam. I hear you're quite a shark."

Adam shrugged. "I do all right."

Four of the brothers surrounded our dining room table next to my father, who placed the cards and the chips in the center. Max pulled a handful of cigars from his jacket pocket and handed them around.

"Hells bells! You got any hell-sticks around here?"

My father looked confused. "Hell-sticks," said David. "You know, matches." My father laughed and put a matchbox on the table.

"Come on, Addie," said Jacob, his eyes bright, pointing to an empty chair. "I'm waiting to win back that twenty bucks you snatched from me last week."

"I won that money fair and square," Adam said.

"Now I'm gonna win it back fair and square."

Adam looked at me. "Do you play?"

"No dames allowed," said Stuart. "They're for playing with when the game's over."

"You don't have to worry," I said. "I'm going to visit my friend Hilde who was fired from her teaching position because she's from Germany."

Adam and his brothers looked at each other but said nothing. I walked to the door and Adam followed me.

"Would you mind some company?" Adam asked. "I ain't got enough dough on me to compete with these chumps. Not you, Mr. Scofield. My brothers, I mean."

As Adam and I crossed streets and dodged pedestrians and automobiles, I noticed the posters plastered on shop windows and lamp posts throughout the city. One poster, in black and white tones, was a drawing of German army boots that read: Keep these off the U.S.A. Buy more LIBERTY BONDS. Another poster had a drawing of a mean-looking German soldier in his pointed hat and a bayonet in his hand that read: Beat back the HUN with LIBERTY BONDS. Another read "Pershing's Crusaders" and showed the leader of the United States Army on horseback leading a troop of strong-looking doughboys in dome hats, an American flag waving behind them with a dream-like depiction of medieval soldiers on white horses in the background, comparing the doughboys of 1918 to the Knights of the Round Table. Now Hilde was without her job, without the income her family needed, and many 100% Americans, if asked, would have said Mrs. Rittenhouse was right to have fired her.

Inside the warmth of the Eberhardts' apartment, life for Hilde's family hadn't yet changed. They had enough savings to get by, for some time anyway. Mrs. Eberhardt, always in her starched white apron, her graying gold hair falling from a high-piled bun, stretched out her ample arms toward me and greeted Adam warmly.

"You are welcome here," she said to Adam. Adam replied in German.

"You speak German!" said Mrs. Eberhardt.

"My brothers and I all do. We learned from our parents, who didn't speak much English when we were kids."

Adam and I sat at the table beside the window overlooking the East River while Mrs. Eberhardt brought in a plate of hot buttermilk biscuits and a pot of coffee. As she served us she explained Hilde was out looking for work. The girlish grin left her heart-shaped face, leaving her looking older than her years.

"Her grandpapa and I are hopeful she will be a teacher again, but she has not been hired yet. We are afraid these other schools are run by people like the Rittenhouses."

"Fools," I said.

"Now, Rose, you know things will work out for the best. My papa, Hilde's grandpapa, will rise from his bed again. Hilde will work as a teacher again, and both of you pretty girls will find nice young men for husbands." She said something in German and winked at Adam, who laughed heartily.

When Adam and I meandered the city maze back to the red-brown brownstone he was lost in thought.

"I didn't know you speak German," I said.

"That's not something you want going around these days with all the stories about what they're doing to the Germans. Did you hear the story about the man who was covered in boiling tar and feathered? Or about the man hanged nearly to his death?"

"What did they do?" I asked.

Adam shrugged. "They were German. That's all. There are too many stories these days with that same punch line, but no one likes to talk about them because they're afraid of being seen as sympathetic to anyone who's German."

"Has it been a problem for you?"

"We've always gotten ourselves into trouble being Jewish and German both. If we were called dirty Jews, or told we couldn't use the same dressing room as the other performers, or chased with blackjacks we were doing okay that day. Usually, it was worse. It's been better since we became the Bell Brothers."

"Since you became the Bell Brothers?"

"When we started in show business we were the Five Meyers Brothers because that's our name—Meyers. We never had it easy being Jewish, but we got our blackjacks and we got by all right, you know, a few scrapes and bruises here and there but nothing serious. When the war started in '14 one theater manager in Arkansas said he wouldn't let any German Jews play for his God-fearing crowd, so Max says, 'What in hells bells makes you think we're German Jews?' and the manager says, 'The name Meyers, for one.' So Max said Meyers was our stage name and the schmuck believed him. That night Max put us on the board as the Hells Bells Brothers."

"I bet the management didn't see the humor in that."

"You saw that poster the night we met. All theaters have the same policy. After all, vaudeville is family entertainment." He snickered at the thought. "We got closed out that night so we figured we'd be better off being the Bell Brothers."

"You should be careful when you play the Palace," I said. "You don't want Max's mouth getting you closed out."

"You don't know the half of it. When acts play the Palace, Albee's eagle-eared scouts monitor everything, making sure no blue material gets performed onstage. If something gets past the censors, it's because of the slyness of the performers who know which double entendres will slide by."

"I suppose that's Max's department to know what you can get away with," I said.

Adam grinned. "True, but even Maxie won't take a chance at the Palace. Some friends of ours played there last year and they said there's a sign backstage that says the theater caters to ladies, gentlemen, and children, and vulgarity won't be tolerated. The sign says to check with the manager if you have any doubt about it, but no one in the business doubts it. Albee's reputation for strictness is known along every vaudeville circuit. If you don't follow his rules, you're closed out of his theaters before you can figure out why. And once he cuts you, he won't ever let you back. Let's just say that man can hold a grudge."

"He has a lot of rules," I said.

"Female performers can't appear onstage unless they wear stockings. Reference to religious differences or physical deformities like lameness, blindness, or serious mental defects are strictly forbidden."

"I agree with that."

Adam nodded. "Those are cheap jokes a lot of small-time acts fall back on to get a quick laugh. We've never made fun of other people in our act. We have enough material making fun of ourselves."

We neared the red-brown brownstone and I was sorry my time with Adam was nearly done. I looked through the living room window and saw my father and Adam's brothers finishing up their poker game, laughing, smoking, and grasping each other's shoulders as though they were lifelong friends. My father looked boyish for the first time in a long while, and I liked seeing him happy again.

"You and your brothers are such free spirits," I said, still watching through the window. "Why would you conform to such extreme rules to perform at one theater when you're loved the way you are across the country?"

"It's like you said, Rose. Albee is the Big Time. You work hard to make sure you're not banished from his kingdom, and if you're good at what you do and you can work within his limitations, then the Palace becomes the path to a rewarding career."

I wasn't surprised when, four days later, my father and I witnessed our friends, the Five Bell Brothers, formerly the Meyers Brothers, knock the audience off their seats at the Palace. The theater itself was no remarkable sight. Sandwiched between low brick buildings—a cheap café, a pool hall, and a music publisher's office—the narrow six-story building had a simple marquee advertising the names of the most-loved performers in vaudeville. I clapped my hands in delight when I saw, in bold letters: Now Playing—The Five Bell Brothers. My father's gap-toothed grin spread from his face to mine and I beamed right along with him.

His grin faded when we walked into the Palace and saw it infected with the Patriotism. Inside the theater was decorated in deep crimsons and gold, continuing the sense of royalty granted to the performers fortunate enough to make it to Albee's stage. Red, white, and blue streamers fell from the ceiling, and the lyrics to "The Star Spangled Banner" were printed in large type in the program alongside an admonishment to report any disloyal comments overheard in the crowd.

My father looked at the chattering patrons and shook his head. "Despite the tax on theater tickets and Heatless Tuesdays, the show must go on."

"Lighten up," I said. "Adam's going on any minute."

My father smiled. "Only Adam?"

I hoped I didn't look as pink as I felt. I set my expression to neutral, but my father knew me too well. He turned toward the stage.

"Before we have the enjoyment of the entertainment of Adam Bell, we have to listen to this nonsense," he said.

The show started with recruiting pitches and propaganda pieces. Yet despite the difficulties brought about by the war, Albee, the Vaudeville King, and his Palace continued to put the best entertainers on its stage, and people flocked to see them. Every seat in the theater was filled, there were sparks of excitement everywhere in the air, and the audience leaned toward the stage when the emcee appeared.

While the brothers performed, their music, their laughter, their laughter in music, the audience buckled over clutching their sides from quake-like hysterics, my father leaned close and whispered, "This is it, Rose. They've made it."

"I hope so," I said.

And my father pretended not to see the smile that lit me up from the inside.

CHAPTER 9

*I*n the spring of 1918, the Great War began in earnest for America as American boys were sent over there in numbers of 300,000 troops a month. Optimism and Patriotism remained intact though fewer male faces were seen crossing the streets or driving cars. Husbands, fathers, sons, and brothers left to lend their support to their bedraggled comrades along the Western Front. Now, the Huns would be beaten into submission, many believed. Now, with American boys assisting their weary French and British allies, the war would find its rightful end.

When American troops began moving across the Atlantic Ocean, my father received a government letter warning him against the pacifism he promoted in his columns. The letter said complaints had been received against him for his "Anti-American" stance. My father was one of New York's most respected journalists, the letter said, and he had a responsibility to direct his readers toward opinions that fostered their Patriotism. My father wasn't acting like a 100% American, the letter said. Still, my father continued to do what he did best, and he wrote his columns anyway.

Then things happened too quickly, like the sputtering, quick-time scenes in the nickelodeons when people moved out of sync with real-life time. One spring afternoon, after I arrived home from school, I noticed that the energy inside felt different. Instead of providing a haven, I heard pleading for the restoration of peace. A sepulcher-like silence engulfed me when I walked past the threshold. Was there an intruder? A burglary? Cynthia and Mrs. Harris were nowhere to be seen, and Molly was hiding under the sofa in the living room. I felt isolated in a ghostly realm while my own home wasn't recognizable to me. Instinctively, I looked for my father. I passed through the kitchen, went upstairs, and without knocking went into his bedroom, but there was no one there. The phone rang and I jumped at the sudden sound loud against the silence. I lifted the receiver, and, trembling, picked up the mouthpiece.

"Rose."

I exhaled when I heard my father's voice.

"Rose," he said, "you need to listen carefully because I don't have much time. I've been arrested. You need to contact Mr. Skimmer." He forced a laugh. "Don't worry. I'll be out by tonight or tomorrow morning at the latest."

"What happened?" I asked. "What's going on?"

"I'm all right. The police officers were very nice, and now I'm sitting in a room with some drunks and pickpockets. I need you to call Mr. Skimmer. He'll know what to do—" He was interrupted, and I heard an important-sounding voice through the line. "I'm talking to my daughter," my father said. "I'm sorry, Rose, I have to go. Call Mr. Skimmer. I love you."

I told him I loved him and, with a shaking hand, hung up the telephone. I searched the piles of papers in my father's office, and I felt the room drop down on me. The fear of enclosure, of free-lessness, the fear that had always been my weakness, was no longer irrational. It was real and happening to my father. I dropped into the wing chair and wept, not only for my father, but also for me. I pictured myself in his place, trapped and unable to find a way out. I saw darkness, dungeons, and airlessness, and I felt the weight of those who had been tied down before me.

I caught myself from falling too deeply into the gloom. I stood and wiped my tears away with my sleeve.

"I can't do this," I said aloud. "I can't stand here and cry. I can't wail or faint or pretend I'm helpless when I'm not. My father needs me."

I was relieved when I phoned Mrs. Skimmer and she said her husband had already been alerted to my father's situation and was working to free him.

"What about the money for the bail?" I asked.

"Don't worry, Rose," said Mrs. Skimmer. "Frank will take care of everything."

Mrs. Harris was late shopping that day, and when she returned I told her what happened. She shook her head and muttered under her breath. She stepped away, turned around, stepped back, and tapped her temple with her finger. "My memory," she said. "It's dreadful getting older, Rose. I used to have such a good memory. What is his name? Your father's friend from college who's a lawyer now. Oh..." She looked physically pained by her inability to remember. "You know how I am with names."

"Mr. Skimmer," I said.

"That's it. Frank Skimmer. You should call him."

"I already did," I said. "He's working on it."

Mrs. Harris muttered more under her breath, nodding and answering herself as she pushed on the kitchen door. She paused as though she forgot what she was thinking, then she turned to me and said, "I'm going to bake one of your father's favorite vanilla cream cakes to have ready for when he returns home. He'll be home soon. I know he will." She disappeared into the kitchen muttering still.

I called Cynthia, who was at her home four blocks away. When she arrived at the brownstone she took my hand and we sat close to each other on the sofa in front of the fireplace, the exact spot where she and my father often sat together into the late hours after other conversations would have dwindled away. When sitting no longer worked for her, she paced the floor in an agitation I wouldn't have expected from her, the woman whose serenity was the goal of my life. Gold hair trickled from her high-piled bun, and her eyes didn't focus while her fingers turned knots in her hands.

Mrs. Harris brought out the tea set, the vanilla cream cake served with whipped cream and strawberries, ready and waiting for my father.

"He'll be home soon," Mrs. Harris said. "I know he will."

We sat, or stood, or paced, or fidgeted, waiting until the sun dropped behind the skyscrapers and the city was a dull, yellow glow, waiting still when the sun left altogether and the sounds of automobiles and El trains passed into the nighttime traffic of restaurant and theatergoers. Even the cat on my lap, nudging my hand with her nose, couldn't hold my attention. Finally, when dawn glowed as a white thought along the dark horizon, my father walked through the door. Cynthia and I ran to him and he hugged us both, then dropped exhausted onto the sofa.

"Frank had to haggle for hours to get bail set for me," he said, "menace to society that I am."

"Martin," said Cynthia, "what happened?"

My father shook his head as if he hardly knew. "Remember that government letter? I didn't heed their warnings." His eyes watered and he looked away. "I know I was just released from jail, and yet I can't believe it's possible to be arrested for expressing opinions in America." His voice cracked under the strain. "I'm disappointed, that's all."

Mrs. Harris brought him a slice of the cake she baked for him, but he had no appetite. Cynthia took one of his hands while I took his other. With my father warm and loved where I could tend to him, I didn't know what to say to ease the silent suffering I felt lingering beneath his quivering shoulders, as if he were still cold though he was far from the frigid jail. My tears fell freely, saying what my words could not.

My father sighed. "This isn't the America I grew up believing in, Rose. I thought we were in a time of great progress, a time when were evolving into something better."

"Some progress has been good," I said. "Women in New York have the vote now."

"You're right," he said, though he didn't sound convinced.

"Think about all the changes we've seen," Cynthia said.

And she was right. The world and the way we lived in it had transformed before our eyes. As I sat there I thought of some of the changes. In 1903, on a North Carolina field known as Kitty Hawk, the Brothers Wright successfully flew an airplane for the first time. In 1908, the first Brooklyn Manhattan subway link opened. In 1909, the Queensboro and Manhattan bridges opened and the Metropolitan Museum held the first show of American art. It wasn't until the first decade of the 20th century that American art was given critical recognition. Before then American art was considered too new to have substance. In 1910, Pennsylvania Station opened, and in 1911 was the horrific Triangle Shirtwaist Factory fire where 146 women and girls were trapped in the jail-like factory and killed by smoke and flames. That same year Irving Berlin's "Alexander's Ragtime Band" made a name for the composer and brought acceptability to syncopated ragtime music among whites who had previously belittled anything associated with Black culture.

1912 was the Titanic disaster, another sign, like the Triangle Shirtwaist Factory fire, that technology wasn't invincible. In 1913, the 60 stories of the Woolworth Building topped the Singer Building as the world's tallest, and the first crossword puzzle appeared in the *New York Sun*. And then, in 1914, the Great War began after years of misguided imperialism, when European alliances remained strong despite the foolishness of it all.

My father closed his eyes. He stayed silent for a long time. He was so still I was afraid to move lest I disturb him. Finally, he said, "I thought we lived in an age of progress, and I thought the progress would lead to better work conditions, better education, better relationships, better equality. Instead, we have a society where the rich get richer and the poor are increasingly neglected and enslaved to their mechanical tasks in these assembly lines or clothing factories. But I couldn't shake my hope for a better future. When the Panama Canal was completed I thought we could make the world better if we concentrated our energies on the same important goals. We can work together."

"You've always been idealistic, Martin," Cynthia said. "When you were courting Eva, that was one thing she always talked about after you had gone and we were left to chat and giggle about you like girls do."

"What did she say?" I asked.

My father turned to me, the surprise in his gap-toothed grin. "Are you asking about your mother?"

"I was just wondering," I said.

"Your mother loved Martin's can-do mentality, his drive to make the world a better place for everyone. Did you know your father idolized Teddy Roosevelt?"

"Why?" I asked.

"He had the radical idea of helping the overworked and under-paid," my father said. "He believed prosperity at any price would destroy America. He put moral principles before self-interests, and he put the welfare of ordinary Americans first. He was irre-pressible, and I loved that about him. I wanted to be the same way."

"He thought people should speak softly and carry a big stick," Cynthia said, laughing.

My father smiled. "Yes, he did. And he was right. You speak your mind, say what you need to say, but be prepared to stand firm when you need to."

"I'd rather use the stick to beat some people," I said.

I pictured Roosevelt, a beefy, bespectacled man who became President after McKinley's assassination.

"He was a hands-on, common man's President who took away the unnecessary ceremony demanded by his predecessors, men who needed to be seen," my father said. "He never would have tolerated the Patriotism. My..." He couldn't say the word. "I never would have been arrested under Roosevelt."

Cynthia gripped his hand. "Martin."

My father shook his head. "I'll be all right."

But he wasn't all right. Suddenly, Martin Scofield, known throughout the city as a man of integrity, a respected journalist and editor, was denounced as an enemy of the American government because he dared to plead for peace. Yet he wouldn't pretend to believe in something he found abhorrent the way he found the unnecessary murder of young men abhorrent.

"We are the adults here," he wrote in what became his final editorial for the *New York Times*. "We are the ones who should understand the difference between right and wrong, who should be teaching our youth the value of compromise, who should be showing how those with differing opinions can live alongside one another without bringing irreparable damage to innocent lives. The bloodshed must end. American boys, or European boys, for that matter, shouldn't be lulled by the belief, by the lie, that what they do is ordained by God when it is the narrow-minded, arrogant wishes of their selfish leaders that send them to the battlefield."

For a few weeks after his arrest, reporters, photographers, and gossips loitered outside the brownstone, wanting a glimpse or a picture of my father, but he walked past with his head high. My father believed the worst of it was behind him, and he could go back to making America the place it should have been but never was. I wasn't so sure, and I was haunted by visions of bar-covered prisons. My father had lived my worst nightmare, confined in a jail, and with a fortune-teller's instinct I felt I would be there too. I wanted to ask him what it was like, being in custody, without choice, at the mercy of others, but I couldn't bring myself to ask. I put the recurring visions of dark, fright-filled dungeons from my mind as swiftly as I could with household tasks, gardening, and brief flashes of wide, friendly smiles and verdigris eyes while soulful piano music filled my ears.

My father's second arrest wasn't so easily dismissed.

"This time," the judge said, "you're simply stubborn, and there's nothing less American than unnecessary stubbornness. Why can't you see this is a noble war? We're helping those less able than ourselves. Why can't you see what every true American sees, that making the world safe for democracy is the right thing to do?"

Then, for added measure, the judge ordered the bailiff to bring the wind-up Victrola into the courtroom where he played "Every Mother's Son Must Be a Soldier" for my father's benefit:

The old Red, White and Blue should mean a lot to you,
My boy, if you're a true American,
For the U.S.A. must stand for justice in our land,
For progress due alike to every man...

My father listened to the lyrics and sighed.

"I must not be a true American, then," he said, "if it means dismissing the principles upon which this country I love was founded."

This time, he spent a week behind bars. This time, his fine was so steep he had to take a second mortgage on the red-brown brownstone that was our protection from just such foolishness in the world. Then he was no longer with the *Times*.

"Did they fire you?" I asked.

"It was mutual," was all my father said.

While he looked for work the only solace I found was at the moving pictures. One film in particular, I can't recall the name, but I remember the rows of cemetery crosses stretching to the horizon, graves packed with fresh mounds of clay dirt. There were airplanes, and people still gasped to see the flying machines as though they hadn't come to terms with the fact that people could soar higher than birds. Then, airplanes were bulky, open-seaters with Ferris wheel propellers flown by aviators in heavy glasses and tight caps. In the film, an American fighter pilot shoots down a German plane with the iron cross on its sides, only to discover he had shot one of his own men. The pilot rushes to his comrade and takes him in his arms. His dying friend absolves him of his deadly error.

"C'est la guerre," the dying man says. It is the war.

The dying man pleads with Jack, the pilot who shot him down, to "stay here with me—for a little." Jack agrees, and then, as his friend draws his last breath, Jack swears he'll get one more "Heine"—one more German—for the dead man. Jack wipes his boots on the German flag with the iron cross, then carries his friend to a horse-drawn wheelbarrow that takes the body to be buried among others.

In the next reels the conquering hero arrives home to a triumphant parade, his plane strewn with flowers. He visits the parents of his dead friend, and the grief-stricken mother breaks down over memories of her son. "I wanted to hate you," she tells Jack, "but I couldn't. It—is—war." Jack falls at her knees in repentance. Later, he admits to his girl, tousle-haired Mary, that he forgot himself with a girl one night in Paris.

"What happens now is all that really matters, isn't it, dear?" Mary asks. The movie ends with a shooting star gliding overhead while Jack kisses the girl he loves. It didn't matter what you did before or during the war, the film said, because you are a new person now that you've survived.

While the newsreels ran I slapped my hand over my eyes, unable to watch the horror of war. Suddenly, there was a new killer, the Spanish Influenza, come to Boston via the military and making its way across the country on the railroad lines. Flashing across the screen were scenes of death from pneumonia, though I felt an odd detachment from it all. I felt sorry for the families touched by the epidemic, certainly I did, but I thought it would never reach anyone I loved. Such illnesses affect others, I thought —the poor, the old, the infirm, so I reacted to news of the flu the way we all react to things that don't concern us, with a shake of the head and a word of sorrow. But I continued with my life.

Two weeks after my father left the *Times*, Montgomery Carter appeared at the brownstone carrying a box for my father, a few of his personal items left behind, two photographs, one of Cynthia and one of me, some pens, and some notes. I took the box from Montgomery Carter.

"Thank you," I said.

Mr. Carter pulled out the photograph of me. His mouth grew wide, which I thought was supposed to be a smile, pitiful though it was. "That was the first time I saw you," he said, looking at the photograph. "I saw this on your father's desk and I thought you were lovely." He glanced around the living room as the kitchen door swung closed and I heard Mrs. Harris giggle. "Are we alone?" he asked.

"We are now," I said.

"Your father isn't at home?"

"He isn't, but I'll tell him you brought these. I know he'll appreciate it."

"How is he?"

"As well as can be expected. He's disappointed, he loved his job, but he wasn't surprised he and the *Times* had to part ways."

"He lost his job because he was stubborn."

"Stubbornness runs in my family." I stood with the box in my arms, struggling to think of some polite topic of conversation, the kind Montgomery Carter's mother was such a master at, but I had nothing to say to him. I wanted him to go away. "Thank you again for bringing these by," I said.

Montgomery Carter dropped to his knees and grasped my hands. I dropped the box, and the papers fluttered around my head while the framed photographs clattered on the floor.

"Miss Scofield, you must forgive me, I know I'm very much out of line, but I cannot rest until I have spoken my mind. I must tell you how I feel."

I tried to pull my hands from his grasp. "Mr. Carter, I'm sure you don't mean…"

"In vain I have struggled, Miss Scofield. It will not do. My feelings will not be repressed. You must allow me to tell you how ardently I admire and love you."

Something about his words echoed inside my head. I was certain I had never been proposed to by Montgomery Carter before—I would have remembered a pitiful scene like this, a young man proposing marriage to a young woman who didn't even care to be in the same room with him—but I knew those words from somewhere. Where? I couldn't think. I forgot about the young man on one knee with my hands in his and closed my eyes, struggling to remember how I knew those lines. I opened my eyes, hoping he'd be gone, that I had dreamed this whole mess and I was saying, like in one of my student's stories, "And then I woke up!"

"Mr. Carter," I said. "Please do get up."

"You haven't said yes, Miss Scofield."

I exhaled, wishing I were anywhere but there in my living room with Montgomery Carter on one knee.

"Said yes to what?"

"To my proposal. You will marry me, Miss Scofield."

It wasn't a question. The directness of his tone, the hard, staring line of his eyes, and I realized. He was telling me, not asking me. You will marry me. Full stop. No question mark anywhere in his sentence. He wasn't asking what I thought of him. He wasn't asking if I wanted to marry him. He wasn't asking if I was willing to give up my teaching, my suffrage work, and anything else in my life for the privilege of being married to a Fifth Avenue Carter. My answer was assumed. You will marry me. You will do what I say. And that is all you will do. Ever. I felt my claustrophobia close in on me, and I saw the walls lean down, ready to crash to the ground as if an earthquake shook them loose. I will never be able to breathe again if I marry this man, I thought. He will strangle my oxygen away.

My stubbornness roared within me, a lioness protecting her pride, and my single-mindedness to live on my own terms shouted war chants in my ears and brandished stakes in my heart. Finally, I broke my hands free from his grasp and escaped to the other side of the room. Montgomery Carter was still on his knee, his hands in the air as though he still held mine.

"Mr. Carter, I'm flattered by your attentions, but I'm sure you don't seriously mean that you want to marry me. My father and I are an ordinary middle-class family. He's a convicted pacifist. I have interests you don't agree with that I have no intention of abandoning even when I'm married. Certainly, there are many young women who will suit your needs far better than I can."

"I agree, Miss Scofield, you're not the best choice. My mother had Miss Cox picked out for me. Her father made his fortune in the paper business..."

"The toilet paper business?"

Montgomery Carter cleared his throat. "The paper business. They're new rich, but they're quite rich, and my mother thought Miss Cox and I were in all ways a good match. In fact, my mother tried to talk me out of you. She told me you're a nearly impudent young woman and your ideas are too modern for an old family like ours. Your family lacks social status, and your father has brought embarrassment to your name with his unpatriotic ways, but once we're married that won't be an issue any longer, I can assure you. You'll have the Carter name to protect you. I simply cannot help the way I feel about you. When I first saw your photograph on your father's desk I knew I would marry you. It took some time to convince my mother, especially after your father's arrests, but she saw I was in earnest and she did come around. She's prepared to teach you whatever you'll need to learn."

"Oh, she'll teach me, will she?" By now I was fuming. "She won't need to bother. I can't marry a man who thinks I'm biding my time teaching and working for the suffrage movement. I can't marry a man who thinks my father is an embarrassment because he refused to give into the idiotic Patriotism sweeping everyone everywhere in the country. I'm in no way humiliated by my father or his actions. He's the bravest, most honorable man I know, and I'm more proud of him and his work than I can express to you right now."

"Those are noble feelings, Miss Scofield, and they show me what I already knew about you—your loyalty knows no bounds. I find that admirable."

I grasped around me, my fingers tapping out a telegraph message in the air, reaching for the right words to make him understand.

"Your mother was right, Mr. Carter. I am a nearly impudent young woman. I don't know how to be any other way, and quite frankly I don't want to be any other way. I'm afraid I'd make you unhappy, as you would make me. It's best if we part as friends."

He didn't leave right away, Montgomery Carter. He sat on the floor, still on his knee, staring at me as though he didn't believe what I said, as though I hadn't yet given him my final answer. As if no one had ever said no to him before. He certainly acted like a man used to getting his way. He didn't look angry when he did finally leave. He looked more like a shell-shocked soldier, like the ones in the newsreels at the Rialto, than a man who had just had his marriage proposal rejected. When he was gone, I locked the door behind him, and opened all the windows, trying to air his presence out of my home. I stared outside at my little garden like I didn't know where I was or why I was there.

Mrs. Harris bustled out of the kitchen, throwing her ample arms around me, and squeezing the air from my lungs. "Did he propose? He did, didn't he? I knew it! I told you the first time he came here you two looked good together. It took every ounce of self-control I had not to peek around the door, but I didn't want to disturb you." She squeezed me even tighter, lifting me an inch off the floor. "Did you set a date for the wedding yet? I'll bake your favorite Boston Cream Pie for the reception and..."

"We're not engaged," I said.

"He didn't propose?"

"I turned him down."

"But why? He's such a nice young man. And wealthy."

"He is certainly wealthy, but otherwise he hasn't much to recommend him, I'm afraid. He's better off with that toilet paper heiress. I'm sure she'd be properly obedient to him."

"Rose."

"I know you're disappointed, Mrs. Harris. You're going to have to trust me. It's better this way."

"You're not getting any younger."

I sighed. "I know, Mrs. Harris. I know."

That night I tried to explain to Cynthia what happened that afternoon, but I hardly knew what to say. I felt like I was trying to describe a scene from a play I hadn't paid attention to and wasn't quite sure who the characters were or the story. I knew Montgomery Carter was in the scene, as I was, but what we said to each other was lost to me. After a few starts and stalls, I finally pieced the scene together in some coherent fashion.

"Tell me again what he said when he proposed," Cynthia said. I repeated Montgomery Carter's words the best I could recall. "Why do I think I've heard those words before?" she asked.

"How odd," I said. "That's what I thought. I've heard those words before."

She followed me into my bedroom and scanned my bookcase. She found the one she wanted, flipped the pages, and laughed aloud when she saw it. She handed me the book and pointed to the words. "Read that," she said.

The book was *Pride and Prejudice* by Jane Austen, and the scene she pointed to was the one where Mr. Darcy proposes to Elizabeth Bennet for the first time: "In vain I have struggled. It will not do. My feelings will not be repressed. You must allow me to tell you how ardently I admire and love you."

I threw the book on the floor and dropped onto the bed. "Montgomery Carter doesn't have an original thought in his head," I said. "He stole his words from a novel?"

"At least he chose a romantic one," Cynthia said. She lifted the book from the floor, closed the cover, and slid it back into its slot on the shelf. "And it sounds like you played your role as Elizabeth perfectly. I would throw a bouquet at you for your fine performance if I had one."

"What performance?"

"You're prejudiced against Mr. Carter's pride."

"His arrogance. And his mother's."

"Exactly. You feel he looks down on you and your family."

"I know he looks down on me and my family."

"But Elizabeth does fall in love with Darcy, and they do marry. Who knows where your relationship with Mr. Carter will end?"

"I know perfectly well how my relationship with Mr. Carter will end, thank you very much. In fact, it's already ended. Besides, Darcy had some redeeming qualities Elizabeth couldn't see when she was blinded by his pride. When Darcy helps Elizabeth's family, he shows he is more than he seems. Montgomery Carter hasn't any redeeming qualities, and I doubt he's more than he seems."

"Are you certain?"

"I'm..." As I thought about it, I realized I wasn't sure. I had only seen him a handful of times. "Do you want me to marry him?" I asked. "Are you going to remind me how old I am, how close I am to becoming a haggard, wiry-haired spinster?"

"I'm merely pointing out the obvious, Rose. Sometimes our first impressions aren't complete, that's all."

A flash of verdigris green blinded me for a moment, and I felt warm from memories of music and laughter. I looked at the Victrola in my room and shook my head.

"I could never be happy with someone like Montgomery Carter," I said. "He's not the kind of man I want to marry."

"Then you shouldn't marry him." Cynthia kissed my cheek. "And that's the end of that discussion."

As I fell asleep that night, I wondered if it was the end of that discussion. I had a feeling, as the darkness overwhelmed me, that I wasn't done with Montgomery Carter and his pride.

CHAPTER 10

y father put out feelers at newspapers and
magazines across New York City, the literary
capital of the country. He saw his unemployment as a temporary
setback and he wouldn't be deterred. He put on his best linen suit,
pulled his derby over his eyes in a self-important way, and
charged into as many editors' offices as he could, to responses that
could be described as cold-shouldered at best. He was too controversial now for anyone to want to take on. At home, he pretended
the loss of his income wasn't worrisome. He wanted to protect me
from what I already knew, that the brownstone was on its second
mortgage and most of his savings had been eaten up in legal
expenses. The free time was a challenge to him but unending to
me, especially since I also wasn't working. It was the dead heat of
a long city summer, and there were no lessons to teach, no smiling
children to take my mind from the difficulties I saw everywhere
around me. Every day for weeks I rang the Eberhardts, holding
my breath while the operator got them on the line, hoping to hear
the smile in Mrs. Eberhardt's voice again and wanting to gossip
with Hilde as we had in less fret-filled times. Finally, I learned that
Hilde was working in a munitions factory on the East Side,

mainly because her family needed the money but also, I think, to prove to herself and everyone around her that she was 100% American, a loyal citizen who would risk her very health to support the war movement in her adopted country.

In August, I returned to school to prepare my classroom for a new year of teaching, excited about my new students and looking forward to the lessons we would learn together. The week before the start of the autumn term Mrs. Rittenhouse informed me that my services were no longer required at her Academy.

"It has come to our attention that parents have learned of your father's situation," she said. "Mr. Rittenhouse has decided that we cannot employ a teacher whose father is a convicted criminal with anti-American views. It isn't good for the children to have such nonsense as a teacher with a criminal parent."

Suddenly, I understood shell shock. I saw myself in one of the wartime newsreels at the Rialto, trapped in the trenches in France, under siege from enemy fire, and I knew what it meant to be bombed with pain-filled gas when you least expect it. I should have expected it. Mrs. Rittenhouse had warned me before, several times. Hilde had already been fired. My father was no longer employed. But somehow I didn't believe it could happen to me the way I didn't believe the influenza epidemic sweeping the country could touch anyone I loved. I turned from Mrs. Rittenhouse a stone-faced mute, as though someone had erased the white-chalk words from the blackboard inside my mind. I wanted to say something wounding, something scathing that would cut to her heart the way her words had cut mine, but looking at her, standing tall, her eyes on the Stars and Stripes, her false sense of propriety, I knew she didn't have a heart to wound. She wouldn't understand.

Without looking at her, or any of the other teachers as they gathered outside my door, I cleared my classroom of my personal belongings, grabbing whatever I could fit into a large box from the closet. I didn't look at them when I walked through my classroom for the last time. I didn't listen to their tittering. I grabbed my box, put one foot in front of the other, and left without a word to anyone. Whatever their comments, I wouldn't know. I wouldn't let them see any reaction from me one way or the other, my expression set in grit.

The tears fell when I was down the block, hauling my heavy box on my shoulder, far from their view. At home I put my box on the kitchen table and looked for someone to talk to but found only Molly curled on the overstuffed wing chair by the fireplace. I went into the backyard but had no patience to tend the garden where flowers showed signs of neglect, their petals wilting, their leaves downcast. Both Cynthia and I had been too preoccupied with my father's trials to give them the care they needed. The flowers looked as downtrodden as I felt, and the sight only added to my gloomy thoughts.

My father, Cynthia, and Mrs. Harris were supportive of me, doing what they could to help me make the best of a bad situation.

"Don't worry, Rose," my father said, though I knew he was counting on my salary to help us while he wasn't working.

"It will be all right," Cynthia said, though she knew that teaching children was the pride of my life.

"Eat something," Mrs. Harris said, though she knew I had no appetite.

For a while I went along with their optimism, but sitting and hoping soon lost its charm and I had an idea that both my father and Cynthia tried to talk me out of.

"You can't work in a munitions factory," my father said. "Do you know how sick those girls get?"

"I need to do something," I said. That was how I rationalized it to myself when I accompanied Hilde to her factory the next day.

The day began badly then grew worse, only to finish on a note of hope that I brushed aside because I didn't know better then. I met Hilde in front of her apartment building and we walked to the large, windowless warehouse along the East River that made murdering war toys like bullets and bombs. Suddenly, I noticed how pale Hilde was. Her sky-blue eyes were unusually large, and she seemed nervous somehow, as if she were too panicked to think a full thought for fear of what that thought might be.

Inside the warehouse was a suffocating darkness alleviated only by the bare electric light bulbs hanging overhead. The first thing I noticed was the stench—acidic and overwhelming. My eyes watered, my lungs burned like I had a furnace in my gut, and I couldn't stop coughing. Hilde wasn't bothered by the odor. She didn't seem to notice it, and neither did the other women working hard at their tasks. These munitions workers had come to the factory for various reasons—some because their husbands and sons were dying abroad and they wanted to do their part for the war movement, others because the work sounded exciting to those who had lived only domestic lives before the war. Others came because they needed the money. The supervisor was Mrs. Dawning, a sweet-natured older woman who talked to her employees as though they were her daughters, and she brought me to a line of young women whose eyes were intent on their own hands because their lives depended on it. The danger of explosions was quite real, and the women had to keep sparks out of the area or risk painful consequences.

The pale-haired, pale-skinned young woman next to me, she was maybe 17 years old, tried to teach me to work the bullet-making machine but I couldn't take my eyes off the women working with TNT. These women breathed in the toxic chemicals for hours every day, which they also absorbed through their skin. After a while they turned golden in color while their hair turned orange. Their bodies were polluted by their work, but the dangers were censored from public knowledge during the war. Few knew the poisonous truth lurking inside the munitions factories. It was only after the war that it became known how the women got sparks and chemicals in their eyes, how they cut off their fingers, and how their limbs were dismembered. People noticed yellow women sitting in trolley cars and walking the streets, but the government insisted the girls were fine, the chemicals weren't dangerous. The young women would take a few days off from work, eat healthy foods, drink plenty of liquids, and all would be well, even if they were yellow. It was only later discovered the women weren't merely yellow but dangerously ill. They were sick for months, and if they didn't die they were often infertile and unhealthy the rest of their lives.

I was at the munitions factory for two hours before I was overcome by the noxious fumes. I felt nauseous, as if I would vomit. The other women worked steadily, focused on the tasks before them, but I struggled to stand upright. I needed fresh air or I would faint. My claustrophobia was too tangible in the window-less warehouse. I made my apologies to Mrs. Dawning and rushed from the shadows into the bright-light sunshine. No matter how I berated myself, no matter how much I knew I needed the money, I couldn't bring myself to go back inside. If I go back in there, I thought, I'll never get out. I'll be trapped in the factory forever. Even the need to keep my sanctuary, the brownstone, safe from bank hands couldn't drive me back. I walked away in my gray smock, my aching head in my hands, dejected and confused.

I've never been prone to fits of depression. I've always found strength in my belief in my right to live on my own terms. But at that moment, running in the opposite direction of the munitions factory, I wondered if it was worth the struggle. What were my terms, anyway? I hardly knew. I walked the streets along the river for a while, turned the corner, and wandered aimlessly around the city, not looking at the faces, not listening to the words they spoke, ignoring the automobiles lurching past at traffic speeds, hoping to find somewhere my mind could rest from the worry.

I ended up far from the factory, turning corners all day. I couldn't bring myself to go home. To see my father in my wretched state would be admitting my failure. What could I tell him? That I couldn't handle even one day in the factory where

Hilde had been working without complaint for weeks? That we had no money coming in? That we were going to be turned out of the brownstone?

Suddenly, money became my obsession. Where to get it? There must be things around the house I could sell. My mother's jewelry, which my father saved for me but I never asked for. Cynthia had money left to her from her husband's death several years before. She would give us whatever we needed, but we couldn't depend on her forever. What if my father never worked again? What if I never worked again? As I walked the city streets, all I saw were dollar signs. I saw $ on signposts. I saw $ on people's foreheads or hats or walking sticks. I saw $ on the sidewalk, one on each consecutive step, and the faster I walked, my hands outstretched trying to try to catch them like pennies from heaven, the faster they moved away.

And then I saw the dark eyes, the dark hair peeking out from under a black derby, the straight shoulders, the uncomfortable smile. I saw him on his knees, asking me to marry him with borrowed words. I heard his mother say, "She will learn."

"What do you want me to learn?" I said aloud.

But then I realized. The Carters had money. If I married Montgomery Carter, my financial problems would be solved. My father's problems would be solved. I wouldn't have to worry about whether or not another school would hire me because of my suffragist tendencies or my father's pacifism. I wouldn't have to worry that my father was considered too controversial to be taken on at another newspaper.

I walked, faster and faster, pushing my way around the people heading in the opposite direction like I was a blind fish swimming against the current. Everything in my life was about doing the opposite of what others expected of me. Was I right about living my life on my own terms, or was I just being stubborn? At that moment, I couldn't see a good thing that had come from my insistence on being independent. Being different for the sake of being different isn't a victory at all, I thought. Maybe Mrs. Carter was right. Maybe I should simply choose a man from the bunch and make the best of him I could. And Montgomery Carter wanted to marry me. I hadn't done a thing to encourage him, but he asked anyway, with Jane Austen's words, but he could have done worse.

Could I be happy with Montgomery Carter? Could I make it work? Every fiber of my being screamed "No!" with such force my brain staggered like a baby's rattle inside my skull, and still I tried to rationalize myself into believing he might be a good match for me after all. I would need to be trained, of course, taught by his mother into obedience like a dog learning party tricks. Sit. Stand. Bark. Fetch. Roll over. Woof.

Maybe Montgomery was more than he seemed, as Cynthia suggested. Maybe I was being too narrow minded, too consumed by first impressions when first impressions didn't always show the full picture of a person. After all, my first impression of Adam Bell had been...never mind. I shook the vision of verdigris-green eyes and sweet smiles away.

I was tired of walking and sat on the curb, out of the way of the people jostling past each other on the sidewalk, far enough from the honking cars in the street. When the thought of Adam came back to me, finding homes for lost kittens or playing the piano, I reminded myself he was an actor, on the road nine months a year, surrounded by beautiful, available women with big smiles. The lure of an actor was strong then, as now. Adam, like his brothers, made no secret of his liaisons, and while he didn't boast about his exploits as his brothers did, he never pretended he was as innocent as his smile would have you believe. Besides, Adam Bell didn't have any money, and Montgomery Carter of the Fifth Avenue Carters had a lot. I need money more than I need friendly smiles and beautiful music, I thought.

It was growing dark and the electric theater lights came on, beckoning the late-time crowds to their entertainments. Still caught up in the migraine-like haze brought on by my haphazard thoughts, I came to a side of town I wasn't familiar with. On the outskirts of the immigrant neighborhood, I saw a beer garden and heard Joplin's "Maple Leaf Rag." I walked inside and saw the saloon filled with hard-looking, working-class men who escaped the reality of their lives with a drink, or two, or ten, at the end of their long days. From the leering glances from some of the drinkers, I felt small and far from home. As women alone tend to do, I searched for the nearest exit and calculated how quickly I could get away, how fast I would have to run to get myself down the block and back up Broadway where the night crowds would be out with their furs, jewels, and studded walking sticks, and I could blend in with the moving bodies until I was home.

The ragtime segued into a Chopin nocturne. I hadn't been led astray at all but brought by design to unruly chestnut and verdigris green. The music stopped and I felt a presence beside me, though I wasn't afraid.

"I'm the dame who slept through your whole act," I said.

When Adam smiled I was happy. He took my hand and led me to the patio where the beer garden was no longer intimidating but inviting. An older, gray-haired gentleman who was either the proprietor or the maitre'd yelled at Adam in German, to which Adam replied in the same language as we walked away.

"I was gonna blow this joint anyhow," Adam said as we left. "Albee can't find me moonlighting here. He fires anyone who works for someone else while under contract with him. Besides, my brothers and I are going back on the road next week."

"The Big Time?"

Adam nodded. "No more five shows a day for us. It's two a day from now on."

The pink-blue sun was nearly gone and the electric lights of the Broadway theaters were on at full strength, glittering against the nighttime sky like fallen wayward stars. Adam led me through the crowds, and we let the shop window displays distract us from any need to talk.

When we were some distance from the theaters and the restaurants, Adam looked at my gray smock with a sideways glance. He fiddled with his pin-stripped suspenders, pulling them out and letting them snap into place. He did this again before tipping his straw hat over his forehead, still watching me.

"I'm disappointed, Rose. I thought you would've told me what's bothering you by now."

So I told him. I told him about my father's arrests, his trials, his time in jail, his fines. I told him about the mortgages on the brownstone, and my father's inability to find work because he was a convicted pacifist. I told him I was fired from teaching, and I told him about my day at the munitions factory. I told him I might marry Montgomery Carter.

"You don't even like him, Rose."

"How do you know?"

"Because I saw the way he was looking at you at your house that afternoon, and you weren't looking at him the same way."

"You don't need to like someone to marry him."

"But it helps, doesn't it?" Adam took my hand in his and tugged me, gently, so I faced him. "Don't do something rash you'll come to regret. You can never be happy with an ass like that. A life of boredom and duty goes against your every instinct, Rose, your very being. I can see in your eyes that you know what I'm saying is true."

Adam brushed my tears away. We stood silently, together, and I wanted more than anything in the world for him to put his arms around me, but he didn't. He did take my hand again, and he led me to Central Park where we sat in the dimmed light on a bench by a pond. He accepted a few pieces of bread from a couple with a young child happy to share. We fed the ducks, and the jostling, hungry beaks cheered me just as they cheered the little boy, whose joy at the birds' fidgety antics was irresistible. When the bread was gone, the ducks moved on to their next benefactors, Adam leaned close to me and asked, "Why are you still feeling sorry for yourself?"

I pulled away. "Didn't you hear a word I said? I have plenty to feel sorry about."

"I know you're having a hard time, but such determination you have. You're living on your own terms, which is more than most people can say."

"Am I?"

"You're not living according to someone else's rules, and that's as close as any of us are going to get to living on our own terms."

"If I marry Montgomery Carter..."

Adam slapped his hand in the air as though he were sweeping Montgomery Carter away into the distance. "You won't marry Montgomery Carter, Rose. You know you won't. Everything always happens for the best. You'll see. Like the time my brothers and I were working one-night stands throughout the Midwest and this theater manager decided he'd pay the Jews, the Five Bell Brothers, half what he paid the other acts on the bill. When my brothers and I protested the manager had his bullies with their blackjacks run us out of town. We were stranded, penniless, and didn't even know where we were. We walked nearly 20 miles through the desolate plains to the next town where we were picked up for a month at three times our usual salary."

"That's a wonderful story, Adam, but my problems are more complicated than that."

Adam stepped toward the street. "I want you should come with me."

I didn't ask where we were going or why we were going there. I followed him down the busy street, past the cable cars to the El station where we climbed the steep steps and boarded the train. Inside was decorated in rich burgundies and heavy draperies, the fine interior a sharp contrast to the shabby exterior. We said nothing as the train jolted its way along the mile-high tracks alongside tall buildings and low-lying clouds. I watched as the newer, taller buildings became more crooked, more crowded, and the further east we traveled the more squalid our surroundings became. Adam watched the tenements we passed through the smudged window. We could see the ordinary, private acts of home life that casual eyes shouldn't see. In gas-lit rooms were women cooking over wood-fire stoves, tending children, folding laundry, serving meals, or sewing. I turned away because these hardworking women didn't need to perform their lives for my entertainment, though the tired inhabitants didn't notice us, commonplace as lack of privacy was for the people with large families in crowded flats.

The entire area extending southward from 14th Street to the Brooklyn Bridge was one vast slum, cluttered with masses of gray, disintegrating tenements in dark, noisy streets with every odor and filth. We weren't so far from my red-brown brownstone, though I felt as if we had taken the El train farther than just blocks, but to another land entirely where everyone, young and old, poor and poorer, had to toil for scraps to eat and innocuous shelter to protect them from the whimsies of the weather. These people, immigrants who passed through Ellis Island strong in their beliefs in the American dream, worked endless hours under legalized slavery in dangerous conditions in sweatshops. Cases of consumption were frequent, as were dismemberments and death. Those who thought technology was only good had to look inside the sweatshops to realize how wrong they were. The mass production of women's dresses gave rise to the needlework industry that gave rise to the sweatshops. Women earned six dollars a week, children three dollars a week.

We got off the El train amidst the tenements and the squalor. Adam led me down a narrow, crooked, pushcart-lined street. He walked with a decisive gait that said he knew where he was going, as if he had walked this path many times. Even at night people sat on the stoops so they wouldn't suffocate in the stifling heat inside the over-crowded buildings. The noises of the slums were still rumbling, the peddlers still calling to passers-by to buy their fish, herring, apples, pickles, scraps of clothing, whatever they had to sell. Women, wives and mothers who needed to feed their hungry families, haggled with the peddlers over the price of the food they desperately needed. These women didn't have the luxury of waiting, as I did. Their children needed to eat now, so they argued, cajoled, cried, begged, shrugged, or feigned indifference—whichever would enable them to bring home barely enough.

Horse-drawn drays navigated the maze of the narrow lanes, avoiding the pushcarts and the elfin boys in suspenders and slouch caps running wild in the streets, the iron-shod hooves clattering over the cobblestones. We passed storefronts with words in Hebrew and English, kosher butchers and bakers. Bearded shopkeepers tipped their hats to Adam, who returned their unspoken greeting. Grocers pulled barrels of coal, herring, and pickles in various stages of pickling into their stores as they closed for the night. We passed tailor shops selling dressmakers' trimmings and second-hand apparel shops with worn-out shoes and jackets hanging in the windows, looking as if they could slide off the hangers and walk away, still holding the shapes of their former owners, still able to speak with eloquence of the sad circumstances that brought a man to sell the clothes off his back. On a block of decaying tenements Adam led me up the stoop of a building with so many fire escape ladders it looked like one vast jail cell, a debtor's prison like those in Dickens' day.

Inside the tenement the stench overwhelmed me the way the odor in the munitions factory had. I slowed as I felt the walls lean closer to me, reaching toward me with secrets I wasn't sure I wanted to hear. I reached out to steady myself, but when I saw a roach move across the stained wallpaper I pulled my hand away and stumbled. Adam caught me.

"You want I should take you home?" he asked.

"I want to see."

And I did want to see. I wanted to understand what Adam

wanted me to understand. We had watched movies together, talked together. I had seen him play piano on and off stage, and it was only then I realized I didn't know him at all though I wanted to.

"If you insist," he said. "You should know about the roaches. We have an agreement, see. I leave them alone, they leave me alone, and everyone is happy."

He took my hand and led me up the stairs since the building was too old for an elevator. We went up a dark, narrow staircase to the fifth floor where children loitered in the hallway, chattering and laughing while their parents yelled at them in Yiddish, Hebrew, or German from inside the flats. There was an iron sink in the hall that served four families, and the only bathroom for the tenants was a clapboard outhouse behind the building and a toilet in the hall on the sixth floor. We reached the flat Adam was looking for and he let us in the open door.

"Pop?" he called. When there was no response Adam looked around the sparsely furnished room. "Pop?" He took off his jacket and loosened his tie. "I bet he's talking with Mrs. Schwartz from across the hall. She's had eyes for him since Momma died."

He gestured to the small couch next to a short table with a vase of fresh flowers and told me to make myself comfortable. I sat next to a chubby red tabby cat sleeping on a nearby chair while Adam disappeared in search of his father. There were no windows in the room, so I opened the door and looked down the hall. There was no sign of Adam, so I kept myself occupied petting the cat.

Finally, Adam reappeared with a genteel-looking, gray-haired gentleman I recognized as the same well-dressed man who led my father and me to the Bell Brothers after I slept through their act. The gray-haired gentleman remembered me the moment I remembered him, and he took my hand with such warmth.

"Scofield!" he shouted. "The daughter of the man who helped my boys so well!"

"Yah, Pop, this is Rose Scofield. Rose, you remember my father, Henry Meyers."

"I remember he was the finest-looking gentleman backstage that night."

Mr. Meyers laughed, nudged Adam, and chattered something in German. After he disappeared into the next room I asked Adam what his father said, but Adam only smiled. He went to the door and gestured for me to follow, and I joined him in the hallway by the window that led to the fire escape steps. We watched the scene beneath us, the urchins still running from steel-helmeted police, the mothers still haggling for bread, the elderly still seated on the stoops outside the claustrophobia. I couldn't believe such lives were lived only miles from my own home.

"You never told me you lived here," I said.

"A lot of fellows in vaudeville are from around here. My mother wanted us to be doctors, see, my father wanted us to open a grocery store, so we compromised and went into show business. We knew a couple of fellows who went into vaudeville—they lived down the block—and whenever they came back they showed up in nice suits, jewels, and shined shoes, and we kids thought acting must be a pretty good game. It wasn't until we started in vaudeville ourselves we found out their jewels were fake, their suits second-hand, and they spit on their shoes before they showed up. But it was a way out, probably the only way out for kids like us."

"But you still live here."

"Just Pop and me. Stuart and his wife are out on Long Island, and the other boys are in the Theater District. I've tried to get Pop to move out, but he said he'd be leaving my mother behind if he left and I can't leave him here alone."

Adam pressed his hands into my shoulders and I leaned into him. A small bird settled into a nest she made for her offspring on the fire escape, and Adam whistled at her and she whistled back in harmony.

"I wanted to show you where I come from," Adam whispered in my ear, his breath a feather along my skin. "I know life is hard for you now, but you need to remember what you have to be grateful for. See those people down there? How tired they look. Every minute they struggle, for air sometimes.

"When I was a kid my mother, may she rest in peace, was one of those women you see haggling or crying or screaming because she wouldn't leave until she had some food to feed us. She sewed for other families until her fingers bled, and my father worked so many odd jobs he lost track of where he was supposed to be in the morning. But even then we knew we were lucky because we had each other. We had sunshine, and we had music, and we had laughter. Whenever my father wouldn't get paid for a job or there was no sewing or the boys and I couldn't find work or we hadn't eaten for a while, my mother would tell us not to complain. When you're feeling down, she said, that's when you get on your knees and say thank you. Thank you to God for this air that I breathe."

I looked at the faces of the women and children leaving the congested streets, and in the shadows I thought I saw monsters jumping out at me. I stopped shivering only after Adam pointed to the gargoyles sitting on top of the buildings.

"Guardians of the downtrodden," he said. "And yet, as dark as it is, this darkness is better than the darkness they escaped from. Over there is an all-consuming darkness, while here, though the shadows are dense in places, it's a hope-filled darkness because lights sprout wherever you look. There's a way out, they know, and even the most tired, the most overwhelmed of them, they know they're on the path toward the light. There's a purpose to their struggles here, and they know their children will do better, their children's children even better, and it's worth the daily struggles because here darkness means possibility where there it's only darkness."

Adam tried to move me back into the flat, but I couldn't stop watching the faces, as though I were watching a feature at the

Rialto where shadows and light unfolded stories about quiet lives of desperation, though this feature wouldn't end in five reels but continue on and on since no one knew how to end it except to let it run out to its foreseeable conclusion. These weren't angry faces or disgruntled faces, but tired faces with pasty complexions, even the youngest of them, their eyes focused on the farthest horizon.

"Their dreams," Adam said. "They're focused on their dreams."

Back at the brownstone, under the glow of the outdoor light my father left on for me, I looked closely at Adam Meyers, any thoughts of marrying Montgomery Carter already a distant memory. I inspected Adam's unruly tangles of chestnut hair and looked deeply into verdigris eyes that didn't look away but looked back, just as curious, and then I didn't remember why I had ever found him unhandsome or average-looking because he became beautiful to me. That night, for the first time, I saw our children in his eyes.

But as soon as I saw the flicker of auburn-haired, green-eyed children I shook the vision away. If I wasn't going to marry Montgomery Carter, who had money, I couldn't marry Adam Bell, who had none. I would find my way out of this mess, I decided. I wouldn't rely on anyone. I wouldn't be a society whore, married because I needed to be financially supported in the world.

I turned off whatever heat toward Adam had begun within me. I thought of the widely smiling ballerina and her equally talented friend surrounding him, laughing, winking, acting coy, shy, or friendly, whichever got the biggest response from whichever man they had their eyes on. Then I thought of Adam, his interest in the pretty blondes rising like two red-lipped kiss marks on his cheeks. I thought of Adam on the road with his brothers, surrounded by hundreds of friendly young women, and I thought he could never settle the way I would want to settle if I were to get married. I wouldn't be like Stuart's wife. I wouldn't turn away, explain away, or pretend away.

Suddenly, the negativity, the self-effacing that women are

trained into from childhood rattled rocks inside my brain. My grandmother's tirades began in my ears, like I was the little girl I used to be, looking for guidance and finding criticism instead:

"Young ladies should be demure when they speak."

"You shouldn't wear that color. It doesn't suit you."

"You're not eating all of that, are you?"

"Smile more."

The Gibson Girl was the ideal in the late 19th century, and she reigned supreme for 20 years. Drawn into perfection by her cartoonist husband, the Gibson Girl was vivacious, capable, and undoubtedly feminine. She was beautiful and tall, and many women tightened their corsets to make their waists Gibson thin. The Gibson Girl embodied the American spirit of the fresh outdoors, always with a tendril of hair escaping the restraint of her pompadour. She was shown driving a golf ball and rowing a boat, and still she was considered the perfect woman. Every girl in America, including me, wanted to be her. There was a time when I would stand as straight as my narrow shoulders would allow so I would seem tall like Irene Gibson, not small like Rose Scofield. There was a time when I played all the sports though I was not athletically inclined. I tried tennis. I tried croquet. I rode a bicycle through Central Park. I wore my starched shirtwaists and boater hats exactly as the Gibson Girl did, but no matter what I did I was still Rose Scofield. The Gibson Girl was voluptuous. I wasn't. She was flirtatious and mischievous. I was neither. She was pinned onto college dormitory walls by hopeful young men. I wasn't in such a category.

I was ten years old at the turn of the 20th century when there was a popular tune called "Daisy, Daisy." I remember singing the words over and over:

Daisy, Daisy
Give me your answer do.
I'm half crazy all for the love of you.
It won't be a stylish marriage.

I can't afford a carriage.
But you'll look sweet upon the seat
of a bicycle built for two.

At the time, I thought it was a sweet song and I reveled in the image of a loving couple forever riding about, both pedaling, working together toward a common destination. A few years later I couldn't hear the song without shirking in revulsion at the knowledge that, to most people, my best hope in life would be to land a good marriage, and it was just a few years after that when I realized my definition of good and other people's definition of good were at odds.

Standing in front of the red-brown brownstone that night, I didn't tell Adam that Montgomery Carter wasn't my first marriage proposal. When I was 21, I was courted by a young man named Anthony Collier, a rising banker in his family firm whose father was an old college buddy of my father's. Though I knew a union with Anthony could never bring contentment or joy, I didn't refuse him immediately. I was surrounded by married women who believed it was their duty to see all women enter into the cult of wifely motherhood. Friends with whom I had spent hours discussing dreams of becoming actresses, dancers, singers, pianists, painters, writers, world travelers, of simply becoming, were suddenly married or keenly intent on becoming so.

I received constant riddling from married friends whose first questions were always, "Have a beau yet?" or "Married yet?" when they knew I wasn't. My unmarried friends fretted about becoming old maids, about their mothers fretting about them becoming old maids, about sisters or friends who were no longer in danger of becoming old maids. They brought up all my fears of being enchained, entrapped, and unable to help myself out into the light.

"It's because you don't have a mother," a friend's mother suggested. "I'm sure your father meant well, encouraging you to have opinions, but he can't understand how difficult it is for women who become spinsters."

Other women, married and unmarried, told me I was crazy to turn Anthony down because for most women he was a life's dream, Prince Charming himself in the guise of a well-tailored dandy, exactly what Mrs. Harris thought Montgomery Carter was for me. When other women were certain marrying Anthony was best for me, there were times I believed them. When I said, "But I have other things I want to do," they cringed. When I said, "But I don't love him," they laughed. The married women said love had nothing to do with it. The unmarried women said love would happen over time.

I had always hoped that somewhere in the world, if not in New York City, was something called true love. I had gone from thinking of love as a foolish thing women wasted themselves over to believing love was the only thing that mattered in marriage. Not the kind that made you feel like you had feathers in your lungs and cotton beneath your feet, like in the moving pictures with Valentino's deep eyes penetrating into your soul, but the kind that, when you look at the person, you know you're looking at your best friend with whom you can share your dreams, your heart, your everything. I didn't believe in love at first sight. That was the kind of love I saw my friends marrying over and becoming unhappy very shortly after the lavishly catered, lushly floral ceremonies where they were princesses for a day. That fairy tale ends too soon. I didn't want a fairy tale.

I did eventually refuse Anthony Collier's proposal. Even then I knew, more than anything, I wanted a friend. I wouldn't find a friend in Montgomery Carter, either. Adam was right. I was not going to marry the Fifth Avenue Carter.

Standing near Adam, even after our bonding hours together, even after he touched me and I leaned into him and we stayed close watching the mosaic of his immigrant neighborhood, even after he walked me home and held my hand, even after I saw a flicker of our children in the prism of his verdigris eyes, I pulled away and said goodnight in the coldest way I could. He stepped back, visibly startled, and he looked into me the way only he could. He was resilient, Adam, like his brothers, who survived a poor childhood and the horrors of small-time vaudeville, like his parents, particularly his mother, a woman who knew the true meaning of gratitude, like whole peoples who came to this country searching for a better way to live and struggled daily to find it. Adam Bell wouldn't be put off so easily.

CHAPTER 11

*M*rs. Rittenhouse had sent out word about me, the daughter of a convicted pacifist, and no school I applied to would hire me. My father was in a similar situation, though his dead ends had fueled him into action in a way he hadn't been in years. He called on friends with like-minded ideals, some writers, some bankers, some advertisers, some accountants, and together they ironed out details for a journal that would welcome contributions from writers who wanted to share their opinions without fear of censorship. My father was lit up again with the excitement of the creative process, of drawing up budgets, calling in favors, and banging on unknown doors just as he had when he was fresh from Yale University and beginning his journalism career, just as Max Bell had banged on his door, bringing the Five Bell Brothers into our lives.

I was caught up by my father's enthusiasm and I became engrossed in the work alongside him, writing letters, reading submissions, telephoning potential investors, and writing my own essays about the problems still faced by women in this century of progress. My father and his friend, Stephen Barrett, a former editor at the *New York World*, were both enthusiastic about my pieces, and they insisted my article about New York women receiving the vote should be included in the first issue of *Scofield's New Review*.

Just as I was becoming used to the idea that I could make important contributions to my father's burgeoning journal, I received a call from Mrs. Belmont, who was ringing from the woman suffrage headquarters in Washington D.C.

"You must come back to Washington, Rose," she said in her lofty voice. "We need you here, and Mrs. Wilcox too. We need to push women's suffrage through at the national level so every woman in the country can vote. Stand and make yourself heard."

When the shock of hearing Mrs. Belmont's voice subsided, I knew I had to go. Suddenly, the old fires burned within me the way they burned in my father, and I was eager to return to the frontlines of the women's suffrage movement. I had to help however I could. For the first time in my life, I had no restrictions or obligations—I wasn't in college, and I wasn't teaching. I was free. I wanted to go to Washington, but then, in a moment of doubt, I decided I couldn't go after all. Adam's words came back to me, loud and right. He couldn't leave his father alone and lonely, and I couldn't leave my father, either, especially since Cynthia had already agreed to go to Washington. But my father knew me so well. When he pried the reason for my unrest from me he led me to my room and helped me pack my bags.

My only regret as Cynthia and I boarded the train at Grand Central Station and waved goodbye to my father as he stood on the platform was that I didn't have a chance to say goodbye to Adam. A few days before I left for Washington, I received a telegram from him saying the Five Bell Brothers were headed out on the Orpheum-time, crossing the country until the season ended the following summer. I tried to keep the disappointment from my face, but I couldn't hide it from my father.

"He'll be back in the summer." My father took the telegram

from my hands and skimmed it. "And he says he's going to write to you."

"I'm sure he will," I said.

My father grinned. "If Mr. Adam Bell happens to send correspondence, I'll forward it to you at your Washington address." I said nothing, though my father knew. Even before I knew, he knew.

As the train lurched away from the station, I leaned my head against the cool window and watched the city flutter past like the final fade out of a film, and then, as I looked around I saw men, women, and children wearing white surgical masks over their mouths and noses, carrying on the ordinary business of train travel while a porter went down the aisle with masks for sale. A gray-haired gentleman traveling with his wife—she was masked, he was not—sat across from us. Cynthia smiled at them in her friendly way and asked, "Excuse me, but may I ask why you're wearing masks on the train? I see everyone else with them and I'm wondering if I should buy one."

"The flu," the wife said, her words muffled through the gauze over her mouth. The woman's white-blue eyes stared over the top of her mask, scanning everyone in their seats, as though any one of them might infect her any moment.

Her husband nodded. "My wife thinks the mask will protect her from the influenza epidemic. I think it's plain silly."

His wife, a distinguished-looking woman except for the surgical mask, cleared her throat in an obtrusive manner, making her dissatisfaction with her husband clear.

"Have you seen the newspaper reports?" she asked.

"When I was at the Rialto last week I saw a cartoon about civilians in gas masks while Germans planted flu germs," I said.

"My husband doesn't take this epidemic seriously, I'm afraid, but I've seen the newsreels of the death carts in Philadelphia hauling away the dead bodies. My sister lives in Boston, and her husband was told by a doctor not to bother feeding his sister anymore because she was beyond hope of recovery. Instead of treating her, the doctor recommended putting her name on a waiting list for a coffin. Caskets are hard to come by these days with so many people dying." She shuttered at the thought. "I read in the paper that this flu turns people blue and black and leaves them raging with fevers, delirium, and bloody pneumonia. The victims' lungs fill with fluid," her voice dropped to a whisper, "and then they drown to death." She glared smugly at her husband. "Tell me again the mask is silly, Hillard."

Her husband shrugged. "You can wear as many masks as you like, my dear. I'll buy you ten more off the porter right now. But I wouldn't wear that ridiculous piece of cloth over my nose if the influenza boarded this train and sat in this seat right next to me." He pointed to the empty seat across from him.

"I wish it *would* sit next to you," his wife said. "Then you'd see how real it is, and I could give it a piece of my mind, scaring peaceful Americans that way. Dreadful flu should stay in Spain where it belongs."

I hadn't yet decided whether or not I should be afraid of this Spanish Flu, but at that moment I was too tired to care. I leaned my head against the window, pretending to be asleep, thinking that if the flu did board the train it would find me unconscious and pass me by.

IN WASHINGTON, Cynthia and I were quickly sent to the frontlines of the war for women's suffrage. Mrs. Belmont, the bouncy flowers on her hat dancing in the quick movements of her head, hustled the Washington workers with the same impatience she had hustled the New York workers. Holding off until the war was over didn't sit well with the women who remained in Washington to continue their silent watch over the White House, calling attention to their cause with the messages on their banners. We are still here, they exclaimed in their silence, their banners held high. We are still waiting.

Much had happened since I was in Washington over a year before. In October 1917, a special session of Congress, the War Congress, passed every measure Wilson recommended. There were laws to protect migrant birds. Forty-seven million dollars were appropriated to deepen rivers and harbors and establish more federal judgeships. Then the lawmakers went home without a thought to woman suffrage. Alice Paul, her stance firm, led 11 women to the White House gates to protest the lack of action taken on their behalf. They were arrested for obstructing traffic, tried, and found guilty. After the women were released there was such public uproar that the suffrage amendment was seen before Congress. Some women thought the waiting was over. They thought they would finally be recognized, though many understood the hardest part had only begun.

I remember my days with Cynthia's serene presence beside me in Washington as a blur of silent picketing outside the White House gates, hours telephoning or writing letters, days spent lettering banners, all our actions demanding the suffrage amendment be given the attention Wilson promised. William Randolph Hearst used editorials in his newspapers to demand action on behalf of woman suffrage, but they were politicians then like politicians now, and acting on behalf of the citizens who needed them most wasn't what drove them. They had to be pulled and prodded to do what common sense should have told them to do. Even the politicians who called Wilson "Kaiser" and "Tzar" or "Autocrat" wouldn't act for the woman suffrage amendment without his approval. Wilson himself had all but abandoned our cause. He had drafted thousands of young American men to make the world safe for democracy overseas, but he wouldn't help the women of his own country. He wanted us to disappear, to slink seamlessly into the distance and give ourselves over to supporting the war effort.

Two weeks after Cynthia and I arrived in Washington, a group of women wearing white dresses and purple, white, and gold sashes stood silently with a banner before the White House. The banner read: *Kaiser Wilson—Have you forgotten how you sympathized with the poor Germans because they were not self-governed? 20,000,000 American women are not self-governed. Take the beam out of your own eye.*

The banner hit a nerve, particularly with young enlisted men eager to fight any enemy they could find. Members of the Army and Navy attacked the women picketing silently in front of the White House gates, and as quickly as the attacks began an angry crowd formed a circle around the unarmed women. The throng moved from the White House, pushing its way across the street to our headquarters, and when they were close enough to our house they began tearing and shredding the banners hanging outside with far-reaching fury. Danger flashed its fists at us from the street outside. They hardly looked like men. Wrath-filled demons flashed their red eyes in our direction, their protruding dry lips shouting obscenities. Lucy Burns, Virginia Arnold, and Elizabeth Stuyvesant ran outside, darted around the furious octopus hands grabbing everywhere at once, seized the remaining banners, and ran inside and up the stairs to hang them from the second and third-floor balconies—out of the reach of the inflamed men, they thought.

I heard the crowd before I saw it. An earthquake-like echo rumbled the floor beneath my feet, and I looked toward the window expecting to see a thunderstorm, a tornado, or some other natural disaster looming overhead. Then I heard the voices, faint at first, farther in the distance, but then louder, louder until I heard the frustrated shouts of their oath-filled words. Suddenly, hundreds of angry faces, some men in their army uniforms, others in their sailor suits, others in street clothes caught up in the rush of the madness, surrounded every side of our house, a human barricade preventing the frightened women from running out and breaking free. I heard the tearing and shredding of the banners and the men's wicked laughter as they slashed, gashed, and bashed our words until they were dirty fragments beneath their feet. After the exterior banners were gone but their frenzy remained, the men pushed their way into Cameron House.

A few women tried to barricade the door, only to be kicked, shoved, and slapped by soldiers and sailors on the doorstep. Two policemen stood on the curb, their hands behind their backs, a lean grin on their faces while they watched three sailors lean a ladder against the side of our house, climb to the second-floor balcony, mount the iron railing, and tear away every banner they saw. With two other women, I raced to the second floor to try to rescue the remaining banners. As I got to the window a sailor punched my friend in the face.

"Why did you do that?" she demanded.

"I don't know," the sailor said. He tore the banner from her hands and jumped down the ladder. I heard a scream, turned, and saw Lucy Burns nearly dragged over the railing by two sailors as she struggled to save the remaining banners.

I helped wherever I could, helping this woman off the ground, tending the bloody wounds of another, and trying to push the front door closed to prevent more intruders from forcing their way in, but the men were too strong and they stepped past me like I wasn't even there. Finally, I turned away, refusing to look at our attackers any longer. I learned at a young age that you can take away other people's power over you by not seeing them. If you don't look at them you can't see their anger, their frustration, their unhappiness, and you can't feel accountable. I knew all along the cause of woman suffrage wasn't popular, but I didn't realize how alone we were until I watched Lucy struggle against her oppressors while the police stood there, amused and unwilling to help.

With a trembling heart, I realized I hadn't seen Cynthia since the riot began. I searched around the bodies in Cameron House and found her in the attic talking to two scared young women who looked ready to faint from fear. I grabbed Cynthia's hand, and pushed my way downstairs over intruders, around intruders, stepping on intruders, I didn't care. I knocked our way through the malevolent crowd, past the unwelcome busybodies in the street, away into the distance where we would no longer hear the foul-mouthed curses. The young women Cynthia had been speaking to followed us, clinging to our skirts as we fled the scene, and 18-year-old Jewel Beauvior burst into tears when she saw the sailors' eyes glowing with cruelty while they ransacked our house. All this because they didn't like the banner they saw the women holding? It didn't make sense. For the first time in my life I felt anger with a scarlet-eyed vengeance, my frustration stemming from the fact that the crazed men would never understand.

Finally, they went away. When there was nothing left standing in the house, our banners all destroyed, our furniture toppled and torn, the women beaten and bedraggled, the intruders disappeared as suddenly as they arrived. The Washington streets outside flowed with their normal traffic. The immediate area around the house was silent without even a whisper of the violence. The men were not arrested or prosecuted, but they did go away, and we were left in the eerie silence to clean up the mess, tend our wounds, and go on to fight another day.

CHAPTER 12

*T*he new bars over the first-floor windows made Cameron House feel like a prison. When I needed to console myself from the incessant feeling that the walls were falling down on me, I thought of the bars as a metaphorical jail representing the prison that had held women captive since the waiting began. Now, after the riot, Alice Paul and Lucy Burns were more determined than ever to end the waiting.

Aren't we doing our part for our country, they asked. Aren't we eating wheatless and meatless, wearing khaki, and sending our sons and husbands, fathers and brothers over there to fight the great fight? Aren't we working outside our homes, away from our families, a mass female exodus into the world to fill the gaps left by the men? Aren't we farmers and elevator operators and mail carriers and traffic cops? Aren't we working sweatshop hours in munitions factories, making killing shells to help our boys win over there? Why are we still unremembered? Because we are women, and women's sacrifices are never noteworthy because women are expected to sacrifice.

After the riot my days were spent assisting Mrs. Belmont. She was a stern-looking woman, her hair dark where it hadn't grayed, and she was well-dressed but not ornate or overdone as well-dressed women can be. Although pushing the suffrage amendment through Congress was her first priority, she was also concerned for those of us young women far from home. Whenever I received letters from my father, Mrs. Belmont took an active interest in their contents. She was impressed with my father's idea for a new journal, and she wanted to contribute however she could—including financially, which my father appreciated.

After a frustrating afternoon of phone calls to condescending, arrogant Congressmen who sounded like they would reach through the wires to pat me on my head if they could, I collapsed on the bed in my room. When I had the strength to open my eyes, I saw the letter left for me on the dresser. I saw my father's handwriting on the envelope and tore it open, eager for news about how his journal was coming along. Instead, I found a brief note from my father along with a longer letter in a hand I didn't recognize. My father's note read simply, "You were wrong." The letter was from Adam.

It wasn't a long letter, not a whole page, and I read it over until I could recite it from memory. The brothers were in Alabama when Adam had written, though they were who knows where by the time I received it. The flu epidemic was severe in the first autumn traces of 1918, and the few patrons who would brave the crowds in the theaters showed up in the thin white surgical masks that were all the rage that season. It was a depressing time for the performers who couldn't compete against illness and death for customers. Adam described how they played in empty theaters, how they were frightened Stuart had caught the flu when his fever wouldn't break, though he finally recovered after three worry-filled days. The brothers wanted to return to New York while the flu faded away, but the other performers on the bill didn't want to lose their headlining act and urged the brothers to stick it out, so they did. Then, at the bottom of the paper, the handwriting smaller and scrawled as though he were writing quickly now, he added that Jacob just received a letter from the government telling him he was drafted into the army. Adam's handwriting became shaky when he wrote the final words.

"Jacob is going to France."

The only comfort I found was knowing that all reports said the Great War had worn out its welcome, and its young men, and must end soon. I hoped the battles would be done by the time Jacob arrived along the western front. Maybe he might never go at all.

Later that night, Mrs. Belmont, Cynthia, and I sat on the stoop outside Cameron House trying to find a soothing breeze during a rare moment when we weren't pestered by lines of citizens, mainly self-important women like Mrs. Carter, picketing us with signs that read "Women Need Not Participate." But that night was quiet. There were no crazed soldiers or sailors, no lookie-loos watching and shaking their heads at us when we appeared outside. The quiet and the solitude were ghost-like, and I kept looking up and down the block waiting for someone to try to take us down. We said nothing while we watched the gold-rimmed sun set somewhere far away, maybe where Adam was, I thought. I pulled his letter from my skirt pocket and Mrs. Belmont looked over my shoulder to see.

"What's his name?" she asked. "And don't ask whose name because you know perfectly well to whom I am referring."

Cynthia answered for me. "His name is Adam Bell."

"Of the Boston Bells?"

"The Yorkville Bells," I said.

Behind us the sunlight reflected off the bars on the first floor windows, making a jail cell on the stoop. Suddenly, I felt panicked and thought I would never be released from the prison that was always following me, waiting for me to make a wrong move so I would fall into its clutches where I should have been all along. You will never live on your own terms, the bars seemed to say as the shadows crept toward me. Mrs. Belmont touched my arm and the fear left and I was again on the stoop in the fading light beside my aunt and friend.

"Are you well acquainted with Mr. Bell of the Yorkville Bells?"

"We're friends," I said. "He's on the road with his brothers now. He's an actor."

"Ah, yes, one of those rogues who traipse into town, steal a young lady's heart, then disappear before anyone asks for an alibi."

"He and his brothers have quite a time with the ladies," I said. "Even his married brother."

"Particularly his married brother?"

"Particularly his married brother."

"So Mr. Adam Bell of the Yorkville Bells is not a married brother?"

"No," I answered. "Adam is unabashedly single and loving every minute of every woman he can find."

Mrs. Belmont nodded. "What kind of actors are they? Do they perform Shakespeare?" I shook my head. "Are they jugglers? Trapeze artists? Dancers?"

"They're funny musicians."

"Don't they play their instruments well?"

"They play quite well, but they tell jokes and do funny things during the performance."

"What does Mr. Bell of the Yorkville Bells play?"

"The piano," I said, "and he plays beautifully."

"Yes," said Mrs. Belmont, fingering the single strand of pearls that fell to her waist, "I'm sure he does."

When the sun was down and the city was dark, we walked back into Cameron House, surrounded by women who could speak intelligently about the revolution in Russia as well as the new world order taking place with the approaching finale of the Great War, which was no longer a new war but a very old one that had to end. I was surrounded by wives, mothers, sisters, aunts, grandmothers, daughters, women who were all these things and still understood that these titles didn't encompass everything they were. These were women who saw themselves in a larger scope than the one already decided for them, only unlike me they learned how to combine all their aspects. I still thought I needed to choose.

"It can be done," Cynthia said as we were lettering banners for our shift before the White House gates. "There are men who understand. I was married to a man who understood until the day he died. Your father understands." She lifted her eyes from the banner to look at me. "Aren't you ever lonely?" she asked.

"No," I said.

"Your father and I were talking about this before you and I left New York. He's afraid he hasn't set the best example for you. He thinks he's shown you that alone is the way to be in the world."

Cynthia's words stumped me because I had never thought of my father as alone. He lived his life as a widower not at all for sympathy. I never thought he wasn't living fully. He was married once, and he loved my mother, and it didn't occur to me that over the years he might be longing for the comfort of loving and being loved in return. My solitary father and my solitary self were together, which meant we weren't really alone. Now I was in Washington, working for a cause I believed in, making friends with women who understood the larger picture of their lives and found pride in their work for the women of their country. When the women who were mothers spoke with loving voices of their children and showed photographs all around, it wasn't to boast of their creations or brag about their possessions. The women who worked for the suffrage movement were wiser than that. They spoke of their children with respect and dignity, as my father had always spoken of me.

"You won't leave your father because you're afraid he'll be lonely," Cynthia said. "Just like you didn't want to come here for the same reason."

"You're wrong," I said, "because here I am in Washington while

Dad's in New York, and we're doing quite well without each other."

"Yes, but you know there will be an end to this and you'll go home again."

I dipped my brush into the purple paint and lettered my "Mr. President, What Will You Do For Woman Suffrage?" banner with a steady hand, one stroke at a time, the way I taught my students to form their block letters in school. Cynthia did the same to her banner in gold.

Finally, I said, "I like having my own life. I like going home at the end of the day and it's quiet. There's no one there expecting me to cook his dinner or wash his socks. I can do what I want when I want. I can read. I can listen to music. I can go to the moving pictures. I can stare at the wall and do nothing at all, and there's no one there to tell me any differently."

"Do you think being married is about cooking someone's dinner or washing his socks?"

"Isn't it?"

"It doesn't have to be. My marriage wasn't like that. Your parents' marriage wasn't like that. If you find the right man, a man who understands, marriage is so much more."

"But I loved teaching, and now I love what I do here. I love writing articles for my father's journal. I love trying to explain why what we do here matters. I can't be weak. I need to do something that makes a difference in the world."

Cynthia put her brush aside and sat on the stool in front of me. "Where did you get the idea that wives and mothers are weak?" I didn't need to answer. "Don't you ever think your mother was a weak woman, Rose. She was weakened by disease. She didn't have a weak spirit."

She came around the table, lifted my down-turned head, and said, "You didn't learn your stubbornness from your father. You inherited it from your mother. If she was here she'd yell about woman suffrage from the highest hill and she'd go to jail and suffer the force-feedings if she thought it would help make equal rights for women a reality." When I began to weep, Cynthia put her arms around me. "You're using your mother's death as an excuse because you're afraid of what might be."

"But how can I be something I've never seen?"

"You can be anything you want to be. You don't have to give up one side of yourself to admit to the other side."

"I don't have another side," I said.

"Of course you do. You're just afraid to look at it. You've outgrown your ideas of yourself and now you're becoming stifled. Let yourself bloom."

"I've already bloomed," I said.

She brushed some stray auburn strands from my eyes and kissed my cheek. "Dearest," she said, "you've only just been planted."

I SEE these young women today who think they're onto something new with their frustration at being designated roles by others. I see them with their resisting frowns and unrestrained hair and I can only smile, nod, and say, yes, I was that young once. Then, we bobbed our hair to free ourselves from the weight of the heavy-piled plaits of our mothers and grandmothers. Today, I see young women burning their bras in the open air, carrying banners of protest, shouting at anyone, waving fists at everyone. Would they be surprised to know that we, too, carried banners of protest in purple, white, and gold? We held our banners like sacraments from God, carried them to the White House, and stationed ourselves before the President. But we didn't raise our fists. We didn't shout. We didn't cry. We stood silently and waited. We knew the men in government, on the newspapers, and in our homes expected us to become hysterical, so we said nothing, our stoicism our best weapon. We didn't burn our bras. To us, the new-fangled self-supporting brassieres were a comfort, a blessing after the corsets and stays we wore as girls, bindings that took our breath away.

In the fall of 1918, the war languishing over there was nearly done, and each day more homes displayed black wreaths on their doors, telling everyone who passed that this was a family in mourning. The Patriotism wasn't as strong as it once had been, and every day more people wondered aloud what it had all been for. Still, we continued to picket the White House with our banners, imploring the President, and still we were ignored.

Increasingly, I left the comfort of Cameron House for sentinel duty outside the White House gates. The sedentary work of letter writing and phone calls began to agitate me. I preferred to stand in the clean autumn air even though the clouds in the sky hovered over us with flannel-faced malice, as though Mother Nature herself was content to keep the women waiting.

Sometimes while on sentinel duty I stood alongside Cynthia, and other times I stood with Violet Nolan, a generous but tough-minded young woman who had a stern way about her dark, handsome features that made her look older than she was. She had nothing but patience, she said, and little of that. Another close friend then was Margaret Brinkeley, a divorced woman at a time when it was scandalous to be divorced. Her husband had several affairs, and while she forgave the first three, the fourth was one too many. To her family she was a pariah because this was a time when people would rather present a false front to society instead of freeing themselves from mistreatment. She reminded me of who I might have been if I married Montgomery Carter, and I was grateful I was there with her in front of the White House gates instead of Fifth Avenue.

After two weeks on sentinel duty, the brisk autumn air began to feel like someone snapping a wet towel at my face. I grew tired of standing in the open, an easy target for passers-by who didn't understand why votes for women were necessary for their own well-being. I was tired of being ignored by the President as he was driven past in his black bubble car, his grandmotherly face intent on speeches and decisions that had nothing to do with the Voting Rights Bill. Wilson's plans were focused on his vision of whole-world peace and a new order that would put the United States of America at the top of the global hierarchy. I still believed strongly in the suffrage movement, but the obstacles were beginning to feel overwhelming and I was tired of waiting.

Then everything changed. One cold day in September, I woke up early and readied myself for another tedious day in front of the White House gates with my picket sign. When the other women and I arrived at 1600 Pennsylvania Avenue I heard a commotion behind us. There were 15 of us picketing that day, and we stood as we always did, stone-faced and unseeing while distant eyes peered at us through White House windows. Though I had stood there many times before, the black wrought iron fence separating us from the colonial-style mansion suddenly looked like the bars of a jail cell to me and I shuddered. Alice Paul was with us that day, her banner higher and straighter than anyone else's. I admired her greatly, but I never felt I knew her well. There was a distance, a coldness to her, and you could feel her staring eyes still watching you even after she turned away. She was a cool strategist, Alice, and no one questioned her authority. Whenever I saw her, her lips were pulled into a tight, flat line, though she never seemed angry, only intensely thoughtful.

Suddenly, like the day of the riot at Cameron House, there was a rumble underfoot and an unsteadiness in the air. The wind blew more briskly, spreading frenzy everywhere it touched. As the commotion grew nearer, I saw a parade of steel-helmeted police officers charging in our direction with their batons raised. Loiterers and passers-by, agitated by the sight of the armed police, started toward us. The leader of the police informed Alice that from that day forward women carrying banners and picketing the White House would be arrested.

"On what charge?" Alice demanded.

"Obstructing traffic," the officer replied.

"We're not obstructing traffic. We're on the sidewalk. The automobiles are in the street."

"If you stay here, you'll be arrested," the officer said.

Alice was calm, composed, as though being threatened with arrest was a common-day occurrence, which it was for her. She had done this too many times before—dealing with police, being arrested, standing before flat-eyed judges, spending time in jail. This was a daily business for her, and the rest of us followed her lead.

"The pickets will go on as usual," she said.

The next day we returned to the White House gates with Alice at our helm. No one bothered us while the messages on our banners proclaimed our thoughts:

England and Russia are enfranchising women in wartime.

The government orders our banners destroyed because they tell the truth.

Mr. President, how long must women be denied a voice in a government which is conscripting their sons?

Chaos ensued the following day when an angry mob stormed us, grabbed our banners, and knocked us around while the police laughed and looked the other way. When the officers had their entertainment, we were handcuffed and driven away in paddy wagons to the sounds of a jeering crowd. Only Violet yelled back at our agitators.

Living out my fear of imprisonment wouldn't begin that day, though. We were put in front of the judge immediately and set free with suspended sentences on the condition that we no longer congregate in front of the White House. We arrived at Cameron House to be saluted as heroes. I was caught up in a new vision of myself as a martyr out to conquer the evils of the world. Cynthia and Margaret, both of whom didn't picket that day, embraced me.

"You're lucky you were released so soon," Margaret said. "Most of the others who get arrested don't get out so quickly."

"It was nothing," I said.

"This time," said Cynthia.

I telephoned my father, and his concern was calmed by the laughter in my voice.

"I heard you were arrested," he said. "I hoped this would be one way you and I would be different."

"I learned my integrity from you," I said.

That night I didn't sleep, invigorated by the adrenaline dancing a two-step beneath my skin. My toes tapped and my fingers snapped with the energy I couldn't settle away. My fear of enclosure became the euphoria of escape, and I felt invincible. The next morning I was ready to go right back to the White House and dare them to arrest me again. Margaret decided to picket with us. I tried to talk Cynthia into coming while she tried to make me stay.

"You won't get away so easily next time," she said.

"There won't be a next time," I said. "They're not crazy enough to arrest us again."

Cynthia shook her head. "This is about embarrassment and injured egos, Rose. That's the worst kind of wrath there is."

But I wouldn't be swayed. I dressed, gathered my banner, and headed downstairs to wait. When I saw Alice Paul that morning I thought she looked more flat-lipped than usual.

"The time has come to conquer or submit," she said. "For us there is but one choice."

We returned to our station outside the wrought-iron fence. The women surrounding me were grim-faced, well aware we were setting ourselves up for something, but I felt myself smiling. Nothing can stop me now, I thought. Somewhere, hidden deep within my most honest truth, I knew I was exposing myself to my darkest fear—being imprisoned and unable to help myself go free —but I had stubborn courage, or maybe it was recklessness, that wouldn't let me back down. I decided to go to the White House, so I must stay. I brushed away the reality with visions of martyrdom. I'll show them, I thought as I stared at the swaying autumn sky. I won't be frightened into doing things their way.

"You will never teach me a thing, Mrs. Carter," I said aloud.

When the police showed up and told us to move, we turned our impassive faces away. Together we could keep each other safe, I thought. But no matter how strong we felt, we were women, unenfranchised, unesteemed, and we were small women compared to the bulk of the police officers who told us, in insulting tones, to be good little girls and go home. When we refused to listen we were arrested again, but this time there was anger in the police as they manhandled us in disgruntled ways, pushed us into the paddy wagons and dragged us into City Hall where we were put into holding cells for two days before our trial. The charges against us? Obstructing traffic.

Slam! Rattle. Clank. The officer shoved us into our cells and turned the lock that kept us trapped inside. In a matter of seconds, my fear became my horror and I berated myself for ever taking this lightly. Oh my God, I thought. What have I done?

I couldn't make a phone call. I couldn't have contact with anyone in the outside world. I was isolated, held away from everyone who loved me, everyone who could help me now that I could no longer help myself. In my panic I pictured my father and Cynthia unaware of my predicament and not knowing where to look for me, not knowing to be concerned, going about their normal lives, fa la la, fa la la, becoming so used to my absence they never even noticed I was gone. The thought of being trapped without anyone knowing where I was brought me to cry silent tears. I put my head on Margaret's lap in the holding cell and gave way to my fear.

Margaret brushed my hair from my forehead the way a mother would tend to her child. "It's all right, Rose," she said. "This will be over soon."

Two days later the sad excuse of our trials began. When I walked into the courtroom my first instinct was to run screaming to the judge, drop on my knees, and implore his mercy. Yet despite my fears I was still proud. The other women with me stood tall and level-eyed, and outwardly I did the same while inwardly scenes of living in terror in a dismal dungeon played behind my eyes. The plan, as related to us by the others, was to force Wilson's administration to make a choice—to allow silent picketing or else suffer the outrage from the American people when they learned of the cruel imprisonment of peaceful women. I thought the plan sounded logical, but this wasn't about logic. Based on what I had seen of public opinion since I had come to Cameron House, I wasn't prepared to trust in the outrage of the American people to set us free.

The judge walked into the courtroom, stern-faced, severe. As he towered above us in his death-black robe he said, his voice as stern and severe as his face, "I feel compelled to take the most drastic means I lawfully can to force these women to obey." We were ordered to pay a fine for obstructing traffic, but we refused since we weren't obstructing traffic. He saw us one by one, single file. Women who were arrested for the first time that day received a sentence of six months imprisonment while the rest of us received seven months.

We were denied our basic rights as American citizens. We had no legal representation. We stood before the judge, and he pronounced his condemnations, and that, as far as he was concerned, was that. Finally, when she was allowed to speak, Alice Paul said, "We are being imprisoned not because we obstructed traffic, but because we pointed out to the President the fact that he is obstructing the cause of democracy at home while Americans are fighting for it abroad. We are political prisoners, and so we must be treated as such." I wasn't surprised when we were denied that too.

The scene in the jury room became fluttery, and for a moment I forgot where I was. When I came back to myself I thought I was slipping away. I looked at my companions and saw their stubborn courage, so I searched for my stubborn courage, which was hiding somewhere deep, so far down I was afraid I wouldn't find it. I did manage to grasp onto it, holding on for dear life, and I knew I wouldn't scream, rant, or faint. I would make my father, my aunt, even my mother proud.

Mary Nolan, a 73-year-old grandmother I had known since my first trip to Washington over a year before, was given six days behind bars while the judge hinted for her to pay the fine. The judge must have had some semblance of a human heart beneath his sepulcher-like robe, and he was afraid jail might be too severe for Mary and might even cause her death. She was a small woman, Mary, and could hardly see the judge over his tall-standing desk so she stood on her toes and said, with halting grace, "My nephew is fighting for democracy in France, offering his life for his country, and I would be ashamed if I didn't join these brave women in this fight for democracy. I should be proud of the honor to die in prison for the liberty of American women." The judge gave her six months in prison.

The pride on Mary's face as she returned to our box reminded me why I was there, but still I felt myself loitering near the edge of a maelstrom. My nightmare had arrived. As I paced the holding cell, Margaret talked soothing words to me I couldn't understand. It was as if she spoke through a telephone with mislaid wiring. I heard echoes of her voice but it was too garbled. Then, as I tried to come to terms with the reality of life in prison, I decided that if I could stand this trauma with my head held high, then, finally, after years of lesser struggles, I would win for myself the right to live on my own terms.

"Look what I've done," I would say when I left the prison, standing tall and daring onlookers to understand. "I helped to make the world safe for democracy. What have you done?"

Those of us who were arrested were supposed to go to the district jail, but we were sent to the Occoquan Workhouse in Virginia instead. As soon as we arrived at the workhouse my resolve to find vindication in my imprisonment dissipated into the stale air. We were herded in, and while waiting for my cell I felt cold and tremulous. I couldn't breathe, not comfortably, hardly at all, because there was a hopeless stench hovering somewhere above my head, as though if I reached upward I could feel the decay that would destroy me.

CHAPTER 13

$\mathcal{I}$ lived alive through a nightmare because I couldn't escape this reality. The shadows of the bars crept toward me, deriding me, letting me know that this was where I belonged. Prison was a whirlwind of senselessness, an endless void without time, without day or night or hours, without contact with the outside world, without companionship or comfort, without clean water to drink. There was no sleep, and it was so cold the only sound I knew besides rattling keys and turning locks was the creaking of my own bones.

Those of us arrested for picketing before the White House refused to do the prison work assigned to us since we were still fighting for the political prisoner status that was our due. As a result, we spent days in solitary confinement in the punishment cells. I could hardly breathe from the foul odors and the bolted windows, and claustrophobia, like two large hands wrapped around my throat, descended on me. It was dark since little light penetrated the crypt-like concrete. I struggled through each day, terrified in a dark, locked dungeon where I slept on a straw mat, ate raw salt pork, and spent hours in the limbo of complete aloneness where nothing existed except my own heartbeat. Onlookers were paraded past my cell, allowed by the warden to peer curiously at me through the bars, shaking their heads at the sight of a caged woman, and when the peeping toms were gone I was watched by the yellow-eyed demons dancing circles in the gloom.

I paced to ease my agitation. I couldn't be still if I wanted to stay sane. I paced from wall to wall and back again until my heels shredded and bled. I left blood puddles on the floor, and I saw the red trails and wondered at my numbness until I continued pacing, pacing, constantly pacing, and then I understood why tigers paced in their cages—the constant movement fooled you into thinking you were doing something about your captivity because sitting there felt the same as letting them win. I wouldn't let them win, the warden, the guards, the onlookers, President Wilson, even Mrs. Carter—all were a force to be overcome in my frenzied thinking. I was stubborn even in my terror. I would suffer the lack of privacy, the putrid meals, the ghouls I saw in the obscurity, the cold and the airlessness, and the constant suffocation I felt in my lungs. My pacing was my way of not staying down so they could point to me and say, "See, she has learned."

I thought of my red-brown brownstone, my father, Cynthia, the picture of my mother on the mantelpiece, and I wanted her to be proud of me. I thought of lives too good to be true like I had seen in the moving pictures, and at times I imagined I was seated in the balcony at the Rialto watching a film about the cruel imprisonment of women whose only crime was wanting to end the waiting. I felt pity for the pale, auburn-haired woman who paced until her feet bled, oblivious to the pain because the cold and her terror of the lurking shadows left her numb. Then I'd hear the metallic rattling of keys or the echoing slam of prison doors and my reprieve would be over and I'd realize with tears streaming down my cheeks that I was the one locked behind the bars, unable to leave, hardly able to breathe. When my grim reality was too hard to bear, I sustained myself with visions of verdigris green, unruly chestnut, and kind, easy smiles. Other times I hummed to myself, finding comfort in songs from better days. Sometimes I repeated Adam's letter over and over to myself as a reminder that there were people in the world who knew me.

The hours blurred one into the other, and I hardly knew whether it was night or light. I don't know how long into my sentence the hunger strike began. One day a voice echoed down the corridor: "Hunger strike, ladies. It's the only way!"

I was hardly eating already, the food was inedible, so a hunger strike wasn't far from what I was used to. I still had a vague notion of being a martyr, so I stopped eating altogether.

As soon as the workhouse guards figured out what we were doing, they jumped into action to prevent us from starving ourselves to death. They descended on me in my cell like maddened hawks on an injured animal, and like the animal I limped away, looking to hide only there was nowhere to go. A matron yanked me to my feet after I stumbled to the ground, and one of the prison doctors shoved a plate of inedible soup beneath my nose.

"Eat this," he ordered.

"No." I turned away.

Two male guards manhandled me onto a stretcher and carried me out. I thought I heard Margaret's voice call after me, but I was too confused to understand.

When I was in an empty, windowless room, the doctor said, "You need to eat something or you'll be sent to the state mental hospital. Do you understand? You're the only one still on a hunger strike. Most of the women are eating again, and those who won't are being sent to St. Elizabeth's. Do you understand? If you don't behave you'll be sent there too." He pointed through the open door to a group of wide-eyed women waiting to be transported to the mental hospital. I shook my head, closed my eyes, and hummed a song from more innocent days:

"Daisy, Daisy, give me your answer do…"

They moved me inside the psychopathic ward with the locked

door and the barred window where a second doctor waited for me. He told me to eat, and again I refused.

Now it was the nurse's turn. "You're the only one still striking," she said. "No one on the outside is helping you, did you know that? Now be a sensible girl and eat something."

I hardly heard their words over the thumping in my chest. Stop! Stop! Stop! my heart cried. Don't! Don't! Don't! The more they tried to cajole me the more stubborn I became. I felt sweat like melted icicles roll down my neck into the small of my back, and then I was so cold my ears shriveled. At that moment the suffrage amendment meant nothing to me. My only intention was to prove my courage to these imbeciles. I was nauseous, and I began to hum again to calm myself.

The matron laughed. "You won't be humming much longer."

Four large prisoners there for other offenses pulled me flat onto the stretcher and held my limbs while the matron steadied my head. Before I knew what was happening the second doctor shoved a wide, thick tube up my nostril, tearing sensitive tissue, and pain-filled firecrackers exploded in my brain. I gasped and gagged, there was nowhere to breathe from, and I thought I would suffocate into nothing. The world went blank while the doctor pushed the tube farther into me as if I were inanimate, a rag doll with no nerve endings, no blood, no pain. I tried to struggle against the invasion, to wiggle, kick, squirm, scream, but the more I fought the more it hurt, so I lay limp and the doctor continued pushing the tube up, up into my raw nose until it fell into my throat. So this is what it's like to be raped, I thought. This is what it's like to die.

When the liquid hit my stomach I vomited. As I drifted in and out of consciousness I saw the doctor leave and I knew the attack was done. So this is what it's like to die.

That night the nurse shined a light into my eyes every hour to see if I had cracked under the strain, but it was the torture of sleep deprivation that nearly drove me mad.

I was force-fed three times a day. Between feedings I paced, hummed, and vomited. Then I grew so weak they kept me in bed in the psychopathic ward. I grew numb to the agony of the force-feedings, the bloody nose, the torn throat, the liquid like air-dropped bombs in my stomach, the retching, the suffocation, all of it meant nothing as I became incoherent to everything except the hallucinations I saw like flickering quick-time nickelodeon pictures. The scenes kept changing, falling in and out of focus. I saw my father carrying on, unaware of my plight. I saw Cynthia living her life as if she had never known me, and I saw my mother's photograph, her dark-haired, pale-skinned image shaking its head at me, disappointed that her daughter had become this helpless, heaving wreck. I saw my red-brown brownstone with bars on the windows, a prison like all the others, no longer a welcoming haven, the flowers in the small garden shriveled and dead. I saw Adam, heard his music, and felt the strength of his smile like warm sunshine on my face after a long winter. I ran toward him, but he turned and walked into the Palace with a beautiful ballerina on each arm, oblivious to me while I waited for him with outstretched arms. In my rare flashes of lucidity I thought I would be there in the Occoquan Workhouse, delirious, nearly mad, forever.

CHAPTER 14

I felt the life-affirming sun on my face, breathed the fresh air, and thought I was hallucinating. I opened my eyes and saw my worried father by my bedside, holding my hand, searching for the external damage done. Cynthia was there too, sponging my sweaty forehead or pouring the glasses of water I couldn't drink fast enough to quench my month-long thirst. I was so cold, and my father covered me with another blanket. I hadn't yet shaken off the delirium I existed in after the force-feedings began, I was running a fever, and at first they feared I had caught the influenza still bringing pneumonia and death across the country. But all I had caught was the blunt end of Wilson's wrath.

In the Virginia hotel with my father and my aunt by my side, clinging to me as though they would never leave me alone again, I knew I was out of prison but I wasn't free. I could still smell the putrid odors, and I could feel the clammy hands of the prison guards as they forced me onto the stretcher and carried me away. How many times had I thought they were taking me to my death, or that I had already died?

In rambling conversations with my father and Cynthia I

learned how we were released from prison on a dare. Public protest was led nationwide by influential women who pointed out that we were being unjustly held, and they promised Wilson would suffer for his actions. The administration capitulated, the prison doors were opened, and we were released after five weeks of a seven-month sentence. Alice Paul was adamant.

"The commutation of sentences acknowledges them to be unjust and arbitrary," she said. "We continue to have one aim: the immediate passage of the federal suffrage amendment."

For the entire five weeks my father and Cynthia kept their silent vigil outside the Occoquan Workhouse. When he learned I was being released my father pushed past the guards and the matrons and other dazed prisoners and found me, incoherent and sickly thin, in the psychopathic ward. He carried me out of the prison, away from the nightmare. As I left the workhouse behind in my father's arms I was too dazed by the blinding daylight to notice the other women who had suffered. I didn't see their haggard faces, their bloodshot eyes, or their haphazard steps. To see them would have been to admit to my sunken depths.

I remember laying in the hotel bed noticing when my father fixed Cynthia a cup of tea or when she touched his arm as he sat by my bed and read to me from the first edition of *Scofield's New Review*. It was too soon for anyone to know if the periodical was a success, but the light behind my father's eyes told me he was hopeful. The war ended two days after I was released from prison, on November 11, 1918, and the great optimism that brought on the Patriotism became the great confusion, which would soon evolve into the great skepticism. The masses, once so proud of the American intention to forge a path toward democracy for the world, were beginning to question what it was all for. Many of our young men weren't coming back across the pond, and many who did were blind, limbless, or suffering such severe nervous agitation they couldn't stop twitching and seeing visions of the trenches and the corpses. Why? was the increasing demand. My father was determined to answer that question, and he believed readers were now, in the wake of their new cynicism, open to his ideas.

When I was strong enough to receive the news, I learned that my beloved father caught the dreaded influenza while on his way to Virginia. He had driven himself in his Model-T, feeling weaker and weaker along the way. He arrived at the hotel where Cynthia was staying and collapsed into the nearest chair, sweating and breathing heavily.

"Cynthia was right there to help me," my father said. "No man ever had a better friend."

I noticed the way they glanced shyly at each other, and I saw Fourth of July fireworks in their eyes. I wanted to applaud this new-found tenderness between the two people closest to my heart. My father looked even more boyish than usual, I thought, the way his gap-toothed grin appeared whenever he checked his appearance in the mirror, the way he looked at Cynthia as if realizing for the first time that she was a beautiful woman.

My father and Cynthia allowed me whatever time I needed to recover. The first week I didn't sleep much because of the nightmares that dropped me back into the dungeon. I shuddered even when I was sitting on the balcony in the sunshine. I saw the doctor with the tube coming toward me when it was only my father wanting to see how I was. At first, the memories were too terrible for words, but my father and Cynthia knew I couldn't move on until I understood how deeply I had been affected by the horror. Finally, in short, stuttered sentences I began to explain what had happened to me, the fear, the force-feedings, how it felt like rape, then numbness, then death, then nothing. We cried together.

The next morning Cynthia brought me my breakfast, I could manage a few bites of toast and butter by then, and she sat by my bed and held my hand. "It will take time," she said, "but there will come a night when you'll sleep without bad dreams."

"I can't forget this," I said. "I need to remember what they did to me. I need to stay strong. I need to stay focused on the goal."

"What's the goal?"

"To win the vote for American women. We'll be victimized by those in power like we were in the workhouse until we can speak for ourselves. I won't succumb to woman's weakness."

"That hasn't changed." Cynthia's eyes grew small in motherly concern. She said, somewhat sadly, "Do you remember when we talked about men who understand?"

"My father understands."

"Yes, he does, and there are other men who understand too. What if you knew one of those men? What then?"

"I won't succumb to woman's weakness."

"Rose, you've already proven you're not weak. Look at what you survived in the workhouse, and you've come out stronger on the other side. What happened to blooming and letting yourself grow?"

"I won't succumb to woman's weakness."

Cynthia sighed and left me alone to think my thoughts.

The next morning I woke up to a voice outside my room, and even in my grogginess I recognized him, soft-spoken and kind. My father cracked the door open and peered around until he saw me looking back at him. He smiled and said, "Rosie, you have a visitor." He stepped aside and there was Adam, his straw hat in his hands, his green eyes looking into mine.

"Hey," he said, his voice morning soft, "you're the dame who slept through our whole act."

I nodded, and then I cried because I already knew what I had to say to him. Adam sat at my bedside, as attentive as my father or Cynthia had been. He poured me water to drink and pulled the blankets closer to my shoulders when I shivered.

"Adam has been in touch with us since you were jailed," my father said. "He saw your name in the paper and had to know how you were."

"As soon as he heard you were released he left his brothers behind and came from Chicago," Cynthia said. She was intent, trying to make me understand. She and my father nodded at each other, then disappeared into the next room. When they were gone Adam took my hands in his.

"Why are you here?" I asked.

"Why, to see you, of course." And then he kissed me.

I relished the softness of his lips, the gentleness of his touch, and then I cried even more since what I had to say hadn't changed. Adam, too, had something to say. He opened his mouth to say it, but he kissed my forehead instead. He thought I cried tears of joy.

He slipped his arms around me, pulling me closer to him, and I pressed into him, touching the tangles of his chestnut hair, sliding my arms beneath his unbuttoned jacket. But then I remembered those hours I wore my heel skin away pacing the steel-barred cell, pacing like a death row prisoner with only hours to live, wanting to make peace with herself and God because there was no time left, no time for anger or confusion because eternity was waving me in.

When I first saw Adam in the hotel that day, his chestnut hair unkempt, his duck jacket unbuttoned, his tie untied, his celluloid collar loose around his neck, his hands in his pockets, when he took my hands and sat next to me on the bed I understood the fairy tale. I knew why girls pretended to mommy their baby dolls and why young women dream of the men they will marry. There was something comforting in his presence, something I had never had and suddenly missed. When he took me into his arms I understood what it meant to be melted by a man. I looked into his honest eyes and lost myself in someone else for the first time in my life. I felt like one of those swooning women I had seen at the moving pictures, their hearts laid out in shades of gray, their soundless beats fainting away after they were kissed, as if they were trapped in the light of their kisser's magnetic eyes. At that moment, in Adam's arms while he kissed my tears away and told me he loved me, I knew there was nowhere else I wanted to be. Which was why I sent him away.

Adam was never good at concealing his feelings. Unlike most of us who pretend to feel nothing, as if it were our destiny to wander through our lives as mere spectators, he never pretended about anything, and his open eyes wouldn't let him hide.

"What do you mean?" He gripped my hands. "I thought you, I thought we…" He shook his head. He didn't understand.

"When I was locked in solitary confinement there was no one there to help me but me," I said. "That's the way it always is. We make ourselves feel better by surrounding ourselves with other people, we allow ourselves to think we can depend on others, but in the end we're on our own."

"That's not true, Rose. When you were in prison we petitioned the warden, and your father hired a lawyer. Max, Stuart, and Dave started a letter writing campaign, and Jakey wrote the President all the way from France. There were a lot of people working to help you."

"But you couldn't stop them until they decided to be stopped."

Adam stared through the window at the drooping late autumn sun. He watched the orange-yellow horizon fade into deep blues, and then the stars appeared, faint against the dark sky. I saw his red-tinged eyes as he searched my face, hoping to see I wasn't really sending him away. But what he wanted to find in me wasn't there. His face dropped, and the smile that could light a moonless night was nowhere to be found. I had broken his heart.

Finally, he said, "A terrible ordeal you've been through. We'll talk again after you're safe back home."

"Go away," I said. "Go back to your smiling ballerinas."

"I haven't been with any ballerinas since that night I walked you home."

"I don't need anyone," I said.

"Rose, please, you don't mean that."

"Like hell I don't. How could you think I would ever be weak enough to love a vaudeville actor who lives on the road and passes women around to his brothers and cheats on his wife?"

"I don't have a wife, but when I do I won't ever hurt her."

I said other things too, hurtful things I never should have said, but I was too caught up releasing frustrations I didn't know what else to do with.

For the next few days Adam knocked on my door and asked to see me. My father or Cynthia would ask if I would see him, and I would say no, and they would tell me why I should.

"He's crazy about you, Rose," my father told me.

"He loves you, Rose," said Cynthia.

It's unfortunate how we can't always see ourselves, and our actions clearly. Only the distance of hindsight allows us to realize how we could have done this differently over here or where we could have listened to those with sound advice over there but we didn't because we thought we knew better. It's our lives, we say, as if we're the queens of our private corners of the universe. We pretend we know what we're doing when really we're sleepwalking, living according to standards that suited other lives at other times, so we live, but not fully because we're not conscious of our actions. I wasn't acting according to expectations for women in the early 20th century, but in opposition to it, which wasn't being true to myself any more than if I had blindly followed what others would have me do. I wasn't listening to my heart because my heart knew something my mind didn't want to accept, and I was so wrapped up in myself I couldn't see the love in anyone else's eyes.

Suddenly, I was very tired. Though I knew there was more work to do for the national suffrage amendment, I had to go back to New York. I had lived on the fringe tips of my nerves for five weeks, and now I needed to see my red-brown brownstone and sit in the over-stuffed floral-patterned wing chair before the fire with Molly on my lap. I wanted to wind up the Victrola and listen to my favorite tunes and look at the flowers in the small garden that I hoped hadn't completely withered away with neglect. Laying in bed, soaking up the sun's weak autumn rays, making up for the time I had been trapped in a dark dungeon, I realized I longed to be home.

CHAPTER 15

The drive back to New York was quiet and uneventful, the three of us lost in our contemplations and concerns. I saw my father and Cynthia sneak peeks at me, checking on me, making sure I was all right. "Do you need anything?" they'd ask me, and I'd shake my head and watch the early winter sky. During that drive I learned what it means to be grateful. I was going home after I thought home had been lost to me forever, and I knew how lucky I was.

The red-brown brownstone became my haven again, except now it was an appreciated haven, not one taken for granted as it once was. I touched the walls like I hadn't seen them for years and I was trying to trigger the memory of what this place had meant to me. As soon as I was in the living room Mrs. Harris ran to me, crying and hugging me and crying some more.

"You're so thin, Rose," she said. "But don't you worry. You won't ever starve again." She wiped her tears with her apron and smiled. "I have your favorite split-pea soup cooking right now." And she bustled into the kitchen to prove it.

When Molly saw me she ran to me like a child seeing her mother after a long absence, and I played with her and her feather on a string until we both slept on the sofa. When I woke up I wound the Victrola and listened to Joplin, but then a sadness I couldn't name overwhelmed me and I shut the turntable off and went outside. I gasped with joy when I saw a hearty little garden, and though it was the beginning traces of winter and there were no blooms, the greenery was healthy in its cold-weather sleep.

My father opened the window, his gap-toothed grin wide. "I started taking care of the garden after you and Cynthia left," he said. "I did a pretty good job if I say so myself."

The rosebushes had been pruned of their blossoms so they could ready themselves for the spring when they would bloom again. As I stood there, the naked, spindly branches began to look lonely, and suddenly I saw sadness in the barrenness. The depression lifted only when I saw my father and Cynthia through the window, sitting in their place before the fire as they had many times before, only now there was an affection in their mannerisms toward each other that pleased me.

With Cynthia helping my father with his journal, I was left to spend my days as I would. I read a lot, mostly Charlotte Perkins Gilman and Kate Chopin, who wrote about women struggling to be themselves. I was particularly attached to Gilman's *The Yellow Wallpaper*, a short story about a young wife who loses her senses dealing with her restrained life and overbearing husband, so much so that she sees a woman trapped in the prison-like pattern of her bedroom wallpaper, a woman who struggles but cannot find her way free. The woman, of course, is herself. Around this time my father introduced me to the poetry of Wilfred Owen, a young man who served in the British Army during the war only to be killed three days before the Armistice. Somehow, a copy of *Scofield's New Review* found its way to London, and a sympathetic British reader sent my father several of Owen's poems published in a newspaper there. In later years, in the Preface to his collection, the world would read in unapologetic words about the reality of the battles over there. "My subject is War," Owen wrote, "and the pity of War. The Poetry is in the pity." We were only beginning to understand.

I wrote a few short pieces for the *New Review* about my experiences at the Occoquan Workhouse, hoping to enlighten those who were still unaware that women suffered such things in America. Other days I sat silent in the garden and looked at the bare rose canes and the dry-looking dirt and wondered how there would ever be life there again, lifting my face to the winter-time sun, soaking up whatever light I could for my own photosynthesis. I told my father I wanted to drive and he handed me the keys to his Model-T. I drove myself around New York City like a tourist in my town, looking at places as if for the first time—down 42nd Street past the ornate New Amsterdam Theater where Ziegfeld's Follies played, past Times Square, past Central Park, around Columbus Circle, down Broadway, past the Theater District, down Fifth Avenue, past Madison Square Garden, around Grand Central Station, along the Ladies' Mile where there was shopping on Sixth Street, down Park Row and past City Hall, alongside the East River Waterfront. I continued into the east side with the tenements and the people, but I turned around when the memories were too hard.

To pass the time I saw many movies that winter, spent many hours in the darkened theater watching the live shows and the newsreels, biding my time until I could be lost in the lives and loves of those in the films and forget my obstacles for a while, forget the headaches I felt as my mind struggled to make sense of everything that had happened. One movie I saw was called *Oh, You Women*, a comedy starring Louise Huff about women who had gone into the world during the war and the problems they faced when the men returned. In the film the topic was handled comically, but in truth when the men came home the women were swept away like annoying flecks of sand in the eye, sent back to their homes as if in disgrace. Thank you, the returning men seemed to say, thank you for keeping our homes, our jobs, and our lives on track while we were gone, but we're back now and your presence is no longer required. Another feature at the time was *Why Germany Must Pay*, about a young man from Alsace-Lorraine who had been drafted unwillingly into the German Army and then forsakes it to seek revenge on the German soldiers who killed his grandfather and raped his sister. The moving pictures were the last to lose the Patriotism.

Perhaps I should have been surprised when, one afternoon later in the winter, I found my way to my favorite balcony seat at the Rialto and found a mass of tangled chestnut a few rows in front of where I usually sat. Adam turned around, saw me, and moved to the empty seat beside me. He said nothing, his eyes fixed on the screen. We sat silently through the end of the film, then walked from the theater together. We were halfway to the brownstone before either of us spoke.

"I didn't know you were home," Adam said.

"I've been home about two months." I could see my breath in rings in the air as we walked along the ice-cold streets and pulled our coats close to our chins.

"How is Jacob?" I asked. The younger Bell Brother was on my mind a lot in the days since the ticker tape parade marched down Wall Street and the white slips of paper fell like snowflakes on the cheering masses. The marching doughboys stood tall in their uniforms and waved at the crowd, pretending they had never lived alongside corpses, never seen horrors, never killed, allowing themselves these moments of joy because they earned them in the trenches. I searched for Jacob under the pyramid-domed hats but didn't see him. "Did he march in the parade?" I asked. Adam shook his head. "He came home, didn't he?"

"Yah, he's home. Most of him anyway."

My hand went to my heart. "What do you mean?"

Adam stared into the distance. "He's shell-shocked. He can't eat. He can't sleep. He wakes up screaming in the night thinking he's still in the trenches. He can't concentrate on anything. I keep telling him it'll be okay. Whatever problems we've had, we've gotten through them. We'll get through this too."

"You come from a strong family," I said. "I'm sure Jacob will be fine."

"I hope so."

We were nearly at the brownstone and I found myself wishing it were farther away. As much as I didn't want to admit it, I missed Adam and didn't want him to leave.

"Isn't it vaudeville season?" I asked. "You guys are usually on the road until summer."

"My brothers are on the road, but I came back. Jacob needs a lot of care right now, and I didn't want to leave Pop alone with him. As soon as Jakey came home I left my brothers on the Orpheum-time in New Orleans." He paused, looking wistfully at the brownstone. "I know my father could have taken care of Jacob, but I wanted to be here to make sure everything was all right."

"The Five Bell Brothers are down to three," I said.

Adam nodded. "For now."

We walked up the stoop and he looked at me, eye to eye, for the first time that day. I glanced through the window into the living room and saw my father and Cynthia on the sofa in front of the fire, sitting so close their shoulders touched and their hands would clasp and let go and clasp again, like schoolchildren afraid of being caught kissing behind the swings.

"I think there's love in the air," I said.

Adam followed my gaze into the fire-lit glow of the living room. "I sure thought your aunt was one cute chick," he said with a mischievous grin. "I'm surprised it took your father so long to figure it out."

"I'm happy for them," I said. "They deserve to be happy."

"Everyone deserves to be happy."

We watched them for a while, then turned away to leave them their privacy.

"Do you think they'll get married?" Adam asked.

"I hope so."

"I'm ready for a family of my own." He was careful to look away from me, his voice casual. "I'm 31 now, and I'm getting envious of the fellows I see with kids on their knees."

He glanced back at my father and Cynthia, a sad, distant look in his eyes. Then he pulled out his pocket watch and checked the time. "I have to get home. Jakey's come to depend on me. There's a lot he can't do for himself now." I thought Adam might cry. "It's hard sometimes, seeing how hard Jakey is on himself, how frustrated he gets, but I tell him he's got to keep trying. What would Momma think if one of her boys gave up without a fight?"

"She'd say to be grateful for what you had," I said.

"Yah, and she'd be right."

Adam disappeared around the corner without looking back. As I watched him I said a silent goodbye to him in my heart because I thought I would never see him again.

CHAPTER 16

*a*fter I recovered enough, Cynthia and I resumed our suffragist tendencies in New York, away from the picketing and arrests in Washington. We resumed our letter writing and telephone campaigns, bombarding senators and newspaper offices with our message. When the 65th Congress reconvened for a final session in December 1918, Wilson included the woman suffrage amendment in his address to Congress for the first time. Then, satisfied he had done his part for democracy in America, he set sail for Paris and the Palace of Mirrors, an elaborate old-time castle reflecting images of bygone days when people aspired to gild themselves. Wilson wanted to assert himself as the chosen one, meant to free the world's oppressed. Again, a vote on the woman suffrage amendment in the Senate wasn't considered. With less than 50 legislative days before Congress adjourned, taking with it the opportunity to pass the Voting Rights Law, something drastic had to be done.

The women in Washington acted. On a misty December day, hundreds of women carrying torches and tri-colored banners went single-file from Cameron House, past the White House, to the edge of Lafayette Park. These honorable women broke every stereotype that had kept them pinned to the fringe of society as mothers, wives, ornaments, whores, prizes, excrescences, virgins, mannequins, and dolls, calling attention to the plight of the American woman. Meanwhile in France, Wilson received a delegation of French working women who urged woman suffrage as one of the points to be settled at the peace conference. Wilson announced his admiration for the women of France and told of his deep personal interest in the enfranchisement of women. It was a grand moment for Wilson as he won a position in the eyes of the world as a devout champion of women's rights. I shook my head in disgust at this blatant disregard for the women in his own country who were once again suffering hunger strikes in squalid conditions, and my heart ached for them. They had been arrested for lighting watch fires, trying to burn away Wilson's hypocrisy. The Voting Rights Law was voted down by one vote, so the fight began anew.

"We're waiting all over again," I said to Cynthia as we sat at the dining room table writing letters to Congressmen we had already written to countless times.

"It's not always a terrible thing to wait," Cynthia said. She was a comforting, beautiful vision in lilac. She stopped writing to adjust some early blooming daffodils in a crystal vase on the table.

It was early spring 1919, the war over, many promises left unfulfilled. Wilson struggled to convince the world there was a need for countries to govern each other, to form a League of Nations as a way to maintain peace and promote democracy. His hypocrisy only added more fuel to our fire. Cynthia and I marched in Alice Paul's demonstration outside a meeting Wilson held at the New York Metropolitan Opera House in one of his many campaigns to encourage the masses to support the League. It was a starry night in March, and we paraded with tri-color banners from our New York headquarters to the Opera House. We were followed by jeering policemen as if we were suspects who had long eluded them. Wielding their batons over their heads, they charged at us and smacked our arms, our legs, and our hands until we dropped and curled into balls with our arms over our heads. Our banners were destroyed before our faces, and the young woman next to me had hers broken over her head. We were trampled, pounded, dragged from here to there, the skin on our arms and legs bruised into rainbow colors. When we were too beaten to continue our protest we returned to our headquarters. The headlines the next morning were inexcusable:

"200 Maddened Women Try to Attack the President."

"200 Women Attack the Police."

I was so frustrated I cried. I walked around the brownstone waving my fist at the wallpaper, stomping on the rugs, angry with anyone who would continue to ignore the truth of our intentions and deny us our dignity. I was ready to give up hope that the Voting Rights Law would ever pass, and, saddest of all, I was ready to stop insisting on living on my own terms. I longed for escape, and the more I drove my father's Model-T around the city the more I thought of packing my bags and driving away to I-didn't-know-where and starting again, a new life that hadn't been shaped by forces out of my control.

A few weeks after the Manhattan riot Cynthia took me to the Cubism exhibit at the Metropolitan Museum of Art. We had lunch at Lindy's on Broadway, then walked into a world I could understand.

I was used to pastel landscapes by Monet or scenic paintings overrun with sunshine yellow by Renoir. Even Van Gogh, whose desolate fields brought sadness, the end of the long, long road, was comfortable to me because there were days when I felt myself alone in his withered world. In Cubism, though, the artists used two-dimensional planes to show objects that were three-dimensional in life, giving the pictures an odd, disjointed look. I looked at Picasso's portrait of Daniel-Henry Kahnweiler from 1910 and I searched the flat planes of the geometrical grid to find the eyes, which were diagonal here, and the nose, which was lower there, his mustache to the side, his hands looking like fans. Georges Braque's "Violins and Palette" was also broken up, mismatched, facing toward me and twisting away at the same time. Depth, proportion, and space meant nothing here. I nodded at the paintings because I knew what it was to be disparate and scattered.

I pointed out Picasso's "Still Life With Chair" to Cynthia. "It's disconnected," I said, "like me."

"These paintings show how things look at first glance," Cynthia said. "When you first look at someone you don't see all of them. First you see their eyes, then their mouths, then their noses. It takes time to focus on the whole person."

I wandered the exhibit arm in arm with Cynthia, searching the grids as if the pictures were puzzles waiting to be put together.

When we left the museum and turned down the noisy city street I recognized an older, dapper-looking gentleman wearing a ruby pin in his tie and carrying a jewel-studded walking stick. He was speaking German to a well-dressed, gray-haired gentleman and he waved when he recognized me.

"Scofield! The daughter of the man who helped my boys so well!"

I introduced Mr. Meyers to my aunt, and he introduced us to Mr. Muller, a producer who wanted to push the Bell Brothers beyond the Big Time and onto Broadway.

"What kind of show will they do?" Cynthia asked.

"A revue," said Mr. Muller. "They'll add bits and pieces of their vaudeville act into a larger show."

"How is Jacob?" I asked. Mr. Meyers' joy dissipated into mist. He stared at his reflection in his shined shoes.

"He is doing the best he can," Mr. Meyers said.

"I'm sorry," Cynthia said. "He'll recover in time."

"This is what we believe."

"How are your other sons?" Cynthia asked.

"They are worried about our Jakey, but they're well." Mr. Meyers nudged my arm as he leaned close. "He's getting married, you know. I don't know why because he's always asking after you."

"I'm very happy for him," I said.

"Yes, yes. She's a nice girl, not Jewish, but what can you do?"

"I'm very happy for him," I said.

We said goodbye and walked toward the brownstone while the city scenes flashed by quick-time around me. The world was blurred, unreal, disjointed like the paintings I had seen, and suddenly I felt unreal and disjointed myself, as if I were waiting to be pieced together. This wasn't how I was meant to be, I thought. I stumbled when I saw the buildings lean toward me, pointing, letting me know I hadn't been released from prison at all. I was still there, trapped somewhere I didn't want to be.

"I won't let you trap me anymore!" I yelled out loud.

Cynthia grabbed my hand and looked into my eyes. "Who is trapping you, Rose?"

"They are," I said, pointing at the skyscrapers, "and they are," I said, pointing at the passers-by as if they were criminals in a line-up. The cars roared past, racing for the moon, and the city sounds made my brain ache.

I saw myself as a Picasso portrait, my eyes here and my nose there, my heart and my mind at opposing corners, never to understand they were on different planes but still part of the same person. I had spent most of my life struggling to be independent, stubborn, and headstrong, but suddenly I saw myself out of place, out of order, out of love. In my fear, as the claustrophobia grabbed the air from my lungs, I forced myself to say the two words that in my ignorance I thought meant weakness.

"Help me," I said.

Cynthia smiled, a strong, serene smile. There was simple wisdom in her manner—a practical sage—and I knew when I was most in need of guidance I had been provided with my own personal angel.

CHAPTER 17

*C*ynthia put me to work in the garden, hoping the lessons would seep in, take root, and bloom through the soil, water, and sun. It was different in the garden now that the war was over and victory gardens were forgotten until the next world war required them again. There were no more nosy neighbors concerning themselves with what we planted, and we were left to sow our own seeds.

Before, when I helped Cynthia in the garden, I did it for the wrong reasons. I gardened flowers because I wanted to prove I could. I didn't like the work. I looked at gardening as a dirty, muddy chore I had to endure to achieve the fragrant blooms I wanted to see in the spring. I covered myself in a hat, gloves, apron, and boots so no offensive dirt would get under my nails or onto my clothes. With Cynthia's guidance, I learned to take pleasure in the process instead of always looking toward the result.

"Gardening is a promise, Rose, not a burden," Cynthia said as she sat beside me. She never used gloves but enjoyed the silken feel of well-tended soil between her fingers. She gazed for minutes at a time at the life-giving earth.

"Look," she said, pointing to budding pink tea roses, "it's

coming to life again. It's had its time to rest, the sun is shining, it's been nourished and watered, and now it's ready to show the world the beauty it's been storing inside."

I marveled at the metal-like rocks lining the border, how the slate faded to charcoal to the palest silver, a metallic sunset I could hold in my hands. I ran my fingers over the rugged edges as they smoothed to round and I delighted in how the mosaic fit perfectly together, like they were meant to be this way, a labyrinth of the grandest design.

"You see," Cynthia said, "things don't need to stay disconnected. Every puzzle can be put together if we take the time to place the pieces correctly."

I looked forward to the gardening, to the hoeing and the fertilizing, the watering, and the pruning. For the first time, I saw the beauty in the act of caring for something else. As I knelt in the soil, all armor but my hat left aside, I talked to the rose bushes and touched their buds and complimented their beauty. I stopped thinking about other things I could or should be doing. I was all right where I was, how I was, and there was nowhere else for me to be but in the garden in the sunshine with the Victrola next to the window playing Mozart while Molly curled into a purring ball beneath the shade of the tree, playing with the shadows of the sun against the leaves. Mrs. Harris brought out glasses of fresh-squeezed lemonade with mint sprigs and chatted about her nephew who was going to Harvard in the fall. So this is what it's like to be at peace, I thought as I snipped some yellow daffodils to bring the summer light inside. This is what it's like to fly.

In the quiet of an evening with my father, my aunt, and Mrs. Harris playing bridge at the dining room table, laughing and talking like this was all there was to know in the world, I finally understood what I had been waiting for. I was waiting for myself. I had been waiting for permission to feel my feelings and act my actions and believe my beliefs, only while I waited I watched myself pass by. I was doing to myself what I accused the world of doing to me, and I was so driven not to be what others would have me be that I neglected to look within to see who I truly was.

Who was I? At 29, I was finally finding out. I was an educated, intelligent, diligent woman who wanted to do well in the world, a teacher not by choice but by design. I contributed with my very life to a cause that deserved the attention of the masses, and I found some success writing about those experiences.

It was with great pride when my father rushed home from his office to tell us in breathless stops what he had heard over the wireless—the woman suffrage amendment finally, after years of failure and frustration, passed the Senate 66 to 30, two more votes than needed. The amendment would be submitted to the states for ratification on June 4, 1919. I cried freeing tears that day. In my heart I knew the amendment would be ratified and women across the country would be able to vote in the national election in the fall of 1920. For the first time since I had come into young womanhood with woman suffrage as my goal, I was left with nothing but time.

I knew, from Cynthia and the extraordinary women I met through the suffrage movement, that it was possible to want and have different things. What I once perceived to be woman's weakness was now to me her great gift—a precious treasure, one that needed to be respected and used wisely but one that was a link between heaven and earth. I couldn't stop thinking about Adam, and even though his father said he was getting married I still wanted to find him and fall on my knees, beg his forgiveness for my arrogance, for pretending I didn't need anyone when there wasn't anyone who can need no one without dying inside. I wanted to tell him I loved him, and I had seen our children in his eyes that night when he walked me home from the East Side, but I couldn't bring myself to go. For all my life lessons, I was still too proud.

But my father knew, and Cynthia knew, and they let me cry freely and didn't ask why because they knew. They knew my thoughts were focused on unruly chestnut and verdigris green. I saw wide, forgiving smiles and slow-moving manners and I heard Joplin and easy laughter. In those moments when I could see and hear nothing else but Adam I cried, more desperately than I ever had before. I was, I thought, a fitting cliché from the moving pictures, a piteous young woman weeping over her lost love.

"It can be wonderful, Rose," my father said as we sat over coffee in the kitchen, the sun glinting winks at us through the window. "Love can be wonderful if you let it be, if you find someone who is wonderful in their way and lets you be wonderful in yours."

But I was still stubborn. I had sent Adam away, and though he resisted he had finally gone to where I couldn't get him back. I had to put ragtime music, moving pictures, funny musicians, poor immigrant neighborhoods, and the gentlest eyes I have ever known out of my mind.

I wanted to return to teaching, but I knew I couldn't return to the Rittenhouses' or any school like it. I wanted to use my talents for some greater purpose than having a classroom and instructing children, necessary though that was. I wanted to go where the children needed me most, where I could make a positive impact in a way only a dedicated teacher could.

In the red-orange autumn of 1919, I began teaching at P.S. 86, located on the East Side where Adam lived. In the summer I showed up at the principal's office without an appointment, and he knew I meant it when I said I had to teach children, I was made to teach children.

Mr. Isaac Silverman was a short, bespectacled young man whose boyish manners made him seem like a student instead of the principal. He shook my hand, offered me a seat, then listened as I recited the facts about my education and experience.

Mr. Silverman looked out the cracked window beside his desk while he tapped his finger to his forehead. "Scofield," he said. "He left the *Times* after his arrests. Is he your husband?"

"My father. After he was arrested for pursuing peace I was arrested in Washington D.C. for helping the suffrage movement. We're a militant family."

I guessed where this was headed. I gathered my handbag and took up my hat, looking for the door and trying to remember my way out. And then Mr. Silverman hired me.

"I grew up in this very neighborhood, Miss Scofield. I worked hard in a factory by day and studied hard in school by night until I could go to college. Believe you me, when I was in college I had plans to settle anywhere but here. The farther from the East Side the better. But then I realized my place was right where I came from so I could help kids like me get the opportunities they deserve." He stood and extended his hand, which I shook. "We need someone who can show these kids they have choices to make and chances to take if they're going to get anywhere in this world." He handed me the keys to my classroom. "Welcome aboard, Miss Scofield."

When the autumn term began I was welcomed by the faculty, young men and women around my age, all idealistic, all teaching for the children, and I knew this was where I was supposed to be. It was a sad-looking school, across from a butcher's where blood oozed from beneath the door and next to the fishmongers market, a gray building with cracked windows and ceilings that leaked in the rain, but it was the finest school I ever knew. I taught 5th grade that year and I enjoyed the older children's intelligence, even if they were distracted by the day-to-day, hand-to-mouth realities of their lives.

When, on August 18, 1920, Tennessee became the 36th state to ratify the woman suffrage amendment, giving the law the 3/4 majority it needed, Isaac and his wife threw a party at their home in honor of everyone who had sacrificed so women in the United States would have their rights as citizens. No woman who fought for the right for representation would ever say her one vote didn't make a difference.

Standing in Isaac's home, I thought of my younger days when my father told me stories about Elizabeth Cady Stanton and Susan B. Anthony, two women who would prove influential in my life. I thought of the time not so long before, my mother's time, when women were little more than unpaid domestic servants with no legal rights, no financial possibilities, no education, no hope. I thought that our new right to vote, now the 19th Amendment of the Constitution, was the end of the long struggle that began in earnest in 1878 at the Seneca Falls Convention. Stanton's meeting with Anthony in 1851 began a 50-year collaboration to end the waiting. Anthony was much on my mind in those days, how she cast a vote in a presidential election and then suffered a trial and prison, how she went before Congress every year for 37 years, from 1869 to 1906, demanding the woman suffrage amendment be passed. She knew failure was impossible though she wouldn't live to see her dream realized. Both women knew the enfranchisement of women was the first step toward creating a truly democratic society where everyone would be treated with political, economic, and social equality. I dreamed that no woman would ever forget that we are lucky to live in a democracy where we have the right to speak out when we think something is wrong with our world. Many women went to jail to make that point. I am proud to have been one of them.

CHAPTER 18

The 1920s were the beginning of the modern era, and the addition of the woman suffrage amendment to the Constitution was only one way the world changed. It was the age of the flapper, and upswept, pompadoured hair was chopped away in favor of bobbed free-flowing styles. Along with shorter hair came leg-baring dresses, turned-down hose, powdered knees, feathered boas, red lipstick, painted nails, and jazz music. The flappers seemed like rebels to their Gibson Girl mothers. They were living on their own terms, and in some ways they were no longer waiting, no longer allowing others to tell them how to be in the world. Men wore fine suits, slicked hair, and fedoras, and the passage of the Prohibition Amendment made alcohol the center of wild, carousing parties in a way it had never been before. Speakeasies were the place to be seen for the smart set as bootleg liquor called to those who would flaunt the law of the land that way. Cynicism was high, selfishness was prime, the age of Patriotism long past, a memory of an old-fashioned time when people believed in things. No one believed in anything any longer except themselves and their own pleasure, and living the fastest, finest life they could after the austerity of wartime was the theme of the day. Margaret Sanger's work to educate women about the advancements in birth control didn't go unheeded, and women were suddenly freer to express themselves in more ways than one.

In April 1920, I turned thirty years old. I was teaching at a school I loved and connected with children who needed me to show them there were scenes for them to see beyond the gloomy slums on the East Side. There was art, and music, and poetry. There was beauty, and there was a good place for them if only they would work to find it. I knew this because I had lived it.

I found my peace. I was no longer struggling with an internal war. I learned patience, and for the first time I wasn't grasping for control. I appreciated each moment, and every day I understood gratitude a little better. I was grateful for my father, my aunt, and Mrs. Harris. I was grateful for their unconditional love and the way they trusted me to find a way to live on my own terms even when I questioned my terms myself. I was grateful for the sanctuary of my red-brown brownstone and for the wind-up Victrola that played my favorite songs. I was grateful for a moment to sip tea, for some time to roll a ball of yarn around with Molly, whose soft, silk-like fur was warm to the touch. I was grateful for a moment to watch the gold-filled sun fade to bronze as it disappeared behind the skyscrapers. I was grateful when my students could read easily for the first time. The comprehension in their eyes was worth any questions we may have had to struggle through. I was grateful when women approached me on the street and said, "I know you were with the suffrage movement and you were very brave."

"Will you vote?" I would ask.

"Yes," many answered.

"Then you will be brave too," I said, "because you're willing to make changes, and that is hardest of all."

Most of all, I was grateful for the little garden and the life lessons it taught from its soil and buds, its blossoms and beauty. My father bought a swing for the backyard, and I took to sitting beneath the shade of the tree petting Molly on my knee, watching the roses sprout before my eyes. They had their innate calendars, gifts from God, and they waited through the darkness for the right time to bloom. I had taken wholly to the symbolic meaning of my namesake blossoms, the way the dead-brown bark, the twisted thorns, and the dry, dormant seeds of winter burst beautifully into fragrant blossoms. I, too, was a rose tugged into a new shape by sun, nourishment, and the promise of beauty.

THE HEAVY HEAT of summer faded into the crisp, clean air of autumn. Multi-colored leaves fell to the ground. The new school year began and children bound their books and walked the blocks to their classrooms where they were given lessons, some grammar, some math, some life. Women across the country voted in the presidential election for the first time that November. Cynthia and I had a grand time as we walked to the polling place and gave our vote against Warren Harding, though he still became the next President of the United States.

A crowd of women huddled together on the sidewalk outside the polling place, and Cynthia and I lingered to talk with a few of them voting that day. Suddenly, I saw how our sacrifices were worthwhile because here was the tangible result of our actions— these women were having their say. I saw Hilde there, placing her vote like the proud American she was. I hugged her, and we talked like no time had passed, no war had separated us, and I knew we would never lose touch again. I hadn't spoken to her since the day I left the munitions factory, embarrassed by my weakness, but Hilde shrugged my fears away.

"This is a good day," she said. "I have my friend back."

I was saddened to hear of Grandfather Rumann's passing that summer. Then I learned that Hilde had married the son of her factory supervisor. She and Richard were living with her mother and they were very happy.

"You're very lucky," I said.

"Yes, I am. But you can be lucky too."

"No," I said. "It's too late for me."

"Don't say that, Rose. When you say something you make it true."

Cynthia and I walked Hilde home that afternoon, then lingered in her new red-brick brownstone only blocks from my own home. We sat over peppermint tea and muffins with lingonberry butter, chatting and laughing while Mrs. Eberhardt's heart-shaped face hovered over us, making sure we ate our fill. I thought I heard Grandfather Rumann's voice, his German accent heavy and not easily understood, telling jokes he learned as a boy. Richard Dawning, Hilde's husband, came home from his work at an accounting house and I saw her joy reflected in his eyes.

A few days later I was leaving the market with Mrs. Harris when I saw a flash of tangled chestnut peeking out from beneath a small-brimmed fedora. I looked around and recognized Jacob Bell standing by the curb, and I knew I had seen Adam. I told Mrs. Harris to go ahead without me, I had seen an old friend, and after she left I went to Jacob.

The closer I got to him the sadder I became. This wasn't the Jacob Bell I knew, one of the Five Bell Brothers of Big Time vaudeville fame who played the Palace and kept audiences across the country convulsed in laughter. This shuddering boy was Jacob Meyers, a doughboy returned from over there with a nerve-twitching shell shock that kept him paralyzed in fear. His eyes darted from here to there, up to down, side to side, watching everything around him since he never knew where the next bomb would drop. He had to see everywhere at once so he wouldn't be surprised. He shook his head like he was saying no, no, I don't want to go through another attack, I don't want to bury another friend, and his hands waved in front of him, creating a barbed-wire barrier between him and the world. He reminded me of a poem by Wilfred Owen, "Mental Cases," about the terror these men saw behind their eyes and couldn't escape.

It was unfair the way people passed Jacob in the street, gawking at first, wondering what was wrong with this quivering young man talking to himself, and then they continued on their way, leaving him behind the same cynical way they left their 100% Americanism behind when the Patriotism no longer suited them. They pretended not to notice Jacob, but they saw him, he was there, broken beyond recognition the same as the young men who lost limbs and faces.

He hadn't seen me since he was too preoccupied watching the automobiles drive past. I touched his arm and he jumped.

"Jacob," I said, stroking his arm, showing I didn't mean him harm, "it's me, Rose Scofield."

He looked blankly at me, struggling to remember from days when he was a carefree boy and life was an adventure. Now that carefree boy was hollow.

"Your dad wrote that review for us," he said finally, smiling when he remembered.

"The Five Bell Brothers are something else onstage. I've never laughed so much."

"I don't go onstage anymore. I keep thinking I see shells in the aisles and corpses in the audience. Not great for a comedy show, you know? I know the shells and the corpses aren't there, but I can't stop seeing them." He turned toward the stop-and-go flow of the traffic, and I had to hold back my tears. "Adam doesn't go onstage now either." Jacob nodded toward the market. "He takes care of me. We moved down the block here after the wedding and Pop's been living with us. A beautiful wedding it was."

"I'm very happy for him," I said.

Jacob glanced through the market window and saw his brother paying for the groceries. "You want you should say hi to Adam? I know he'd want to see you."

"I have to go." I kissed Jacob's damp cheek. "I want to see you onstage with your brothers again soon."

"I'll try in February. That's when we go to Broadway."

I glanced back only once, to see Adam with a box of groceries in his hand while Jacob pointed in my direction. I knew Adam recognized me because his expression changed. I walked faster until I was running away from him, running from things I thought I could never have, my tears branding me with sorrow.

When I ran up the stoop of the brownstone, away from the verdigris green I couldn't bear to see, I dropped to my knees and looked up at the darkening sky, feeling like I was falling down, like I was back at the workhouse on a stretcher when they carried me away to where no one would ever find me again. When I felt as low as I had ever felt, I looked up, raised my hands to the sky, and said thank you, thank you to God for this air that I breathe.

THE NEXT AFTERNOON I arrived home from school to find my father sitting alone in the living room with the shades drawn low and the electric lights off, a thoughtful fire burning in the fireplace. It was winter, and the sun slept longer. My father looked at the photograph he held in his hands. From across the room I saw the picture of my mother, the one hidden away and ignored for too long. Before I could say hello Mrs. Harris bustled in with a steaming teacup filled with orange pekoe, cream, and two sugars the way I liked.

"I thought you might like this," she said, handing me the cup. "It's cold tonight." I savored my first sip, allowing the liquid to warm me inside.

Mrs. Harris clasped her hands under her chin and her eyes widened. "He was here, Rose! He came asking for you!"

"Who?" I asked.

"You know...the young man. You know."

"I don't know, Mrs. Harris. What's his name?"

"His name?" Mrs. Harris twisted her apron around her fingers. "Oh, Rose...you know how I am about names." She shook her hands in the air like she was strangling the unnamed man. "What was his name?"

She looked at my father for help, but he only shrugged. "I wasn't here at the time," he said.

Mrs. Harris scurried away, shaking her head and twisting her apron again. "Don't worry. I'll remember. But he was here, Rose. He was here for you." As she disappeared into the kitchen I sighed.

"It must have been Montgomery Carter," I said. "I received a letter from him the other day congratulating me for the passage of the suffrage amendment."

"He certainly took his time. It passed months ago." My father looked at the clock on the mantelpiece. "You're late tonight."

"There was a faculty meeting, and then I had some papers to grade."

He nodded, then returned to the photograph—my mother's level eyes, the set mouth, the strength underlying the dark-haired beauty.

"I never realized how much you look like your mother." Red rings circled my father's eyes. "There are a lot of things I never realized. I should have told you about your mother, Rose. I shouldn't have let you go all these years without knowing her."

"But I didn't want to know her. I thought she was weak, and I didn't want to be weak."

"And I knew it too. I knew you thought your mother was weak, but it was too hard for me to talk about her. Every time I thought about your mother I thought I would never stop weeping. I didn't want you to see me that sad. I didn't want you to hurt the rest of your life, feeling like something was missing."

"But something was missing."

"Yes, but I didn't see it that way at the time." He handed me the photograph and I saw what he saw, a vibrant young woman consumed too soon. "Your mother knew exactly what needed to be done and was able to do it. Yet beneath that strength was this serenity that touched everything around her."

"Like Cynthia," I said.

My father paced the length of the living room. He looked through the window at the faded streaks of rain filtering from a tired sky.

"You like Cynthia, don't you?" he asked.

"I love her. She's been my angel."

"She's been mine too."

He pulled a small box from his trouser pocket and showed me the filigree emerald and diamond ring. "I'm going to ask her to marry me. But only if it's all right with you. Only if you'll give us your blessing."

I kissed his cheek, my silent consent.

"I want you to know, Rose," my father said. "I wasn't always in love with Cynthia. When she came back to New York after her husband died I appreciated her companionship and I knew she was good for you, but over time I realized what an extraordinary woman she is, how secure, how resilient, how beautiful. I began to love her as more than a friend, but I thought I was doing better by your mother by feeling half-empty inside instead of keeping her memory alive with my joy."

"That changed in Virginia," I said.

"I was so sick from the flu, and as I recovered I realized even more strongly than when your mother died how precious time is. I'm a lucky man, Rose. I've known three extraordinary women who have added so much to my life—your mother, your aunt, and you."

I began to cry. My father put his arm around me, but he let me cry and didn't make me explain. For that moment I thought there was nowhere for me to go, no dry land to climb onto where I could help myself from drowning.

"Don't follow the example I set all these years," my father said, his voice soothing, as if I were his motherless baby girl again.

"Don't be proud. Go to him. Tell him you love him. He loves you, Rose. I've seen it in his eyes."

"It's too late," I said.

"My dear, if you've learned anything from me you know it's never too late if you're honest about how you feel."

"No," I said, sobbing through my words, "it's too late. He's married." My father's surprise was evident in his open mouth. "His father told me he was getting married, and then I saw Jacob yesterday and he said it was a beautiful wedding."

My father shook his head. "Even if he is married, at least now your heart is open so the next time you meet a nice young man..."

My sobbing became so strong I gagged and heaved while my air pipes closed and my lungs shut down and I felt like I was being force-fed again for reasons I didn't understand. For years I thought I had no heart, I was too cold to love anyone, but suddenly I realized I had a heart, a large one. I knew because the sorrow I felt like a puncture wound in my chest was nearly unbearable.

In January 1921, my father and my aunt married in a simple ceremony at our red-brown brownstone, creating a small circle of love that would last whole lifetimes and beyond. When Cynthia took my hands in hers and said between her joy-filled tears that now we were truly a family, I understood what it meant to belong somewhere, and on that day I gained what I always wanted but wouldn't admit to—a mother. I knew the loss of my mother could never be made up for, but here was a wonderful woman who could not only fill the space reserved for Mother in my heart but could tell me more about the one I lost. I began to crave stories about her, this woman named Eva Scofield who looked like me and acted like me and loved me so much.

The loose threads in my heart were being knotted and ended one by one. After the wedding I lived a life of quiet contemplation, grateful for the simple joys I shared with my family. I found serene satisfaction in the more gracious route my life had taken. I learned to appreciate the gift of living when I was able to say thank you, thank you to God for this air that I breathe.

It didn't pay to replay the past, I thought, like watching old newsreels trying to figure out where events had gone wrong and wondering what could have been done differently. I could only do better in the future, so I left Adam Bell in the background of my mind, though he was always there as laughter, kindness, and music. I contented myself by observing the loving happiness between my father and my aunt, my parents now, and between Hilde and Richard, who now had a little girl to call their own. I resigned myself to watching love from the fringes, and whenever I felt lonely I reminded myself that I was loved once by a kind, honest man with the most beautiful green eyes and a smile that could light the tallest skyscraper in the city. That would have to be enough for me, I thought. I would have to find other dreams to comfort me when I closed my eyes at night.

CHAPTER 19

*I*n the early days of 1921, the buzz around New York City concerned the Broadway reunion of the Five Bell Brothers. People everywhere seemed to know about them, having seen them in vaudeville and loved them. My private knowledge was now shared all around.

I remember the night when my father pulled me into a dilapidated second-rate theater and I fell asleep in the warmth of the audience, only to go backstage to meet some funny musicians who made me laugh and had to be brothers. They had made their name, they had found their place, and I was left to reminisce about scenes I thought were never meant to be.

One evening in February my father came home with three tickets to the theater, and my parents and I went to dinner and onto the Casino Theater on Broadway and 89th Street. As we neared the corner I saw the electric light marquee proclaim: The Five Bell Brothers in TOGETHER AGAIN. I turned around, needing to get away, but my father took one arm and Cynthia took my other arm and they marched me into the theater as if I were a nearly impudent child who wouldn't mind her manners.

We were shown by an usher to seats next to the aisle in the second row, and I shrank close to the floor.

"I don't want to see him," I said.

"It's the Bell Brothers," my father said, his gap-toothed grin wide. "They're the funniest act in town."

I didn't feel like laughing. Cynthia took my hand and nodded in encouragement, but I was too agitated. My old bouts with claustrophobia returned and I thought the theater was falling in on me. Then the emcee appeared, explaining how this was the first show the Five Bell Brothers had performed together in three years. The audience cheered its appreciation. The curtain went up and the five of them stood there, even Jacob, who wasn't as bright as he once had been though he remained level-eyed as he surveyed the audience. When he saw nothing to frighten him he laughed, a beautiful laugh that set the tone for the whole evening. He saw me and nodded, and when I nodded back I prayed Adam didn't look my way.

Time was suspended in that joy-filled land of music, nonsense, and laughter. The brothers goofed around most of the show, but now they were onto the serious part because whenever Adam played the piano the mood changed from frivolity to earnestness, as if that man and that piano were all alone in the world, dependent on each other for their lives. He performed beautifully, his eyes closed, oblivious to the rest of us while he played a sublime melody. It was a slow tune, a Chopin nocturne, and tears streamed down my cheeks while I watched him. I wanted to be in that paradise too, though I had resigned myself to watching from the audience only to go home to wait to be entertained another day.

Suddenly, from where his brothers sat during his solo, a lone voice called so loudly it rang to the balcony and bounced back to the stage, "Ain't that the dame who slept through our act?"

The theater went silent when Adam stopped. I shrank lower into my seat when he stood from the piano and searched the crowd, but it was hard for him. The bright lights in his eyes made the people look like voids behind a black velvet curtain.

"Where? Where?" Adam asked.

"There," said Jacob, pointing at me.

"Rose?" Adam called.

When Adam called my name my father pushed me into the aisle and up toward the stage. "I'm here," I said, but Adam couldn't hear me. The words were caught somewhere inside.

As if on cue, the overhead lights came on, Adam saw me, and he jumped from the stage. He took me into his arms and whispered, "I love you, Rose. From the day I brought you home to the East Side I've loved you."

I had to choke out my words. "I've loved you since the day you played piano at the brownstone."

"Then why did you send me away?"

"Because I was stubborn."

Adam laughed. "Ain't that the truth. Even after I visited your house you wouldn't see me."

"When did you come?"

"A few weeks ago. Your housekeeper said she'd tell you I came by."

I smiled at the memory of poor Mrs. Harris flustered and knotting her apron between her fingers because she couldn't remember my gentleman caller's name. But then I remembered Mr. Meyers words, and Jacob's, and I stepped away.

"But you're married!" I said.

Adam looked toward the stage and nodded at Max.

"He's the one who got married, to a girl named Mary Lou."

"But I thought…"

"If I'm not married to you I'm not married to anyone."

From the stage, over the oohs and aahs from the audience, came a loud "Well, hells bells! Kiss her already!"

Adam kissed me amidst the enthusiastic cheers from the audience. Happy tears spilled down my parents' faces, and the four brothers onstage serenaded us. In a flash of enlightenment I knew I was no longer waiting. There was nowhere else in the world for me to be and no one else for me to be with.

WE WERE MARRIED in June 1921, and our first daughter, Eva Cynthia, was born a year later. She was named for both my mothers, my first mother and my second mother, firmly entrenched in my heart, my two halves made whole. Adam treated his family the way he treated everyone in his life, with kindness, compassion, and humor, and I was the only girl whose smile he cared for from the day we found each other again.

Since Adam's passing I've taken to spending hours looking over the scrapbooks I've collected over the years. I have one of the woman suffrage movement in parades, sentry duty, and rallies. It reminds me how far women have come in many respects and how far we still have to go for the utopia I dreamed of where we would be allowed to be ourselves without apologies. I still have the thick black book Max Meyers Bell hauled into my father's office, and there, never to die or fade away, are the faces of five young men who had to be brothers, who smiled for the world and each other, who brought us all along their merry ride, and everyone who saw them lived happier for it. I have my wedding album, my groom smiling contentedly, as if he knew this was how it was going to be all along. I have an album for each of my three children, my two daughters and my son, Eva, Rebecca, and Martin, charting their progress through the years as they grew into people I was proud of.

Sometimes, I find the irony of me, the headstrong, stubborn one, living the life I had been taught to believe in all along, not because others expected me to but because I was able to do it on my own terms, which were honest and fair. After my marriage I remained a teacher, a writer, a gardener, and a fan of the moving pictures. I was a daughter and a friend who became a wife and a mother. I became a woman, a complete woman who understood how her different facets formed one great gem that left life colorful in its brilliance. My road to victory wasn't simple, but then our travels are never easy to navigate. To be forced along someone else's journey is to ignore our self-knowledge, and only we can know what is right for ourselves.

After I agreed at my granddaughter's insistence to write down my story, I wondered who would be interested in an old woman's ramblings about days when world wars were new, when optimism was traded for a pessimism we haven't yet recovered from, when automobiles, electric lights, telephones, moving pictures, and airplanes were marvels of technology, when women were beginning to make appearances in the world, but then I realized that I can share what I've learned.

And what is it I've learned? I've learned about following your own road despite the detours, when everyone else gives misguided directions, when you think you've made a wrong turn and lost your way, when suddenly you turn an unexpected corner and find a garden, a glorious bounty of fragrant blooms that speak to the beauty you've been searching for all along and you know you've arrived, that this is your victory. I wanted to share my own words of hope for those who are still waiting.

AUTHOR'S NOTES

As always, first thanks go to my amazing readers from all over the world. Since *Her Dear & Loving Husband* was first published, many of you continue to inspire me to keep writing. Thank you.

Victory Garden was inspired by a news report about how people of voting age, particularly younger voters, are not voting. My thoughts immediately turned to the decades-long struggle for women's suffrage. We've come a long way, baby, due in large part to the brave women who dedicated their lives to making votes for women a reality. Each time I step into a voting booth, I am grateful to these women.

When I was growing up in New York, my uncle Bruce Arenstein introduced me to laughter in the form of the great vaudeville comedians—including Abbott and Costello, Laurel and Hardy, the Three Stooges, W.C. Fields, and my all-time favorites, the Marx Brothers. In fact, the Bell Brothers are loosely based on the Marx Brothers. Thanks, Uncle Bruce.

If you'd like to learn more about the American women's suffrage movement, you could begin here: *Sisters—The Lives of America's Suffragists* by Jean H. Baker and *A Woman's Crusade* by Mary Walton.

Portions of *Victory Garden* have appeared in *The Maxwell Digest* and *Muse Apprentice Guild*.

ABOUT THE AUTHOR

Meredith Allard is an award-winning author known for the bestselling *Loving Husband Trilogy* and the Victorian novel *When It Rained at Hembry Castle*, which IndieReader named a Best Historical Novel. Her prequel, *Down Salem Way*, earned the B.R.A.G. Medallion and was a semi-finalist for the Chaucer Award in Early Historical Fiction.

A recognized authority on the craft, Meredith is the author of *Painting the Past: A Guide for Writing Historical Fiction*, a #1 Amazon New Release in Authorship and Creativity Self-Help. For over twenty years, she has mentored writers of all ages, helping them find their voices while honing her own signature blend of meticulous research and haunting prose.

When she isn't unearthing the secrets of the past, she can be found in the hills of Southern Nevada with her cats and a cup of coffee.

Join Meredith online at www.meredithallard.com for her weekly blog posts and monthly newsletter.

BOOKS BY MEREDITH ALLARD

And Shadows Will Fall

Christmas at Hembry Castle

Down Salem Way

The Duchess of Idaho

Her Dear & Loving Husband

Her Loving Husband's Curse

Her Loving Husband's Return

Painting the Past: A Guide for Writing Historical Fiction

The Professor of Eventide

The Swirl and Swing of Words: Embracing the Writing Life

Victory Garden

When It Rained at Hembry Castle

Woman of Stones